A civil engineer by profession, Mohanachandran went on to become the GM of a reputed MNC in Dubai. He established an Indian school which has become one of the top schools in the UAE over the last 30 years.

His first book '*Can My Life Be of Any Assistance*?' was published by The Write Place in 2016 and second book, '*If I Could, You Could Too*' was published by Troika Books in 2017. Both are motivational books. The self-help book is intended to inspire the young generation who are from the myriad villages in India. His hobby is writing.

Mohanachandran T.

SINGLE MOTHER

AUSTIN MACAULEY PUBLISHERS™

LONDON • CAMBRIDGE • NEW YORK • SHARJAH

Copyright © Mohanachandran T. (2020)

The right Mohanachandran T.to be identified as author of this work has been asserted by him in accordance with Federal Law No. (7) of UAE, Year 2002, Concerning Copyrights and Neighboring Rights.

All rights reserved. No part of this publication may be reproduced, stored in a retrieval system, or transmitted in any form or by any means, electronic, mechanical, photocopying, recording, or otherwise, without the prior permission of the publishers.

Any person who commits any unauthorized act in relation to this publication may be liable to legal prosecution and civil claims for damages.

This is a work of fiction. Names, characters, businesses, places, events, locales, and incidents are either the products of the author's imagination or used in a fictitious manner. Any resemblance to actual persons, living or dead, or actual events is purely coincidental.

The age category suitable for the books' contents has been classified and defined in accordance to the Age Classification System issued by the National Media Council.

ISBN – 9789948347491 – (Paperback)
ISBN – 9789948347484 – (E-Book)

Application Number: MC-10-01-6935360
Age Classification: 13+

Printer Name: iPrint Global Ltd
Printer Address: Witchford, England

First Published (2020)
AUSTIN MACAULEY PUBLISHERS FZE
Sharjah Publishing City
P.O Box [519201]
Sharjah, UAE
www.austinmacauley.ae
+971 655 95 202

ACKNOWLEDGEMENTS

Smitha Menon, my daughter, for cover page and for valuable suggestions.

Fauzia Anjum, my efficient secretary, for typing out the story.

Sobha Mohan, my wife, and son, Ashok, for motivating me.

Aditya is an engineering student entering his prefinal year. He is from an aristocratic agricultural family. Nitya is in school doing her grade 10 examination. She is a girl from the fishing village near the engineering college. An accidental meeting turns into a love story. Assisted by Aditya, the first rank grade 10 girl becomes a top ranked student in the college while excelling in sports too. The final day before Aditya leaves after completing his engineering course, the two love birds become victims of uncontrolled emotions.

Both pursue their academic careers far from each other and become highly successful. But by a quirk of fate, the unwed mother Nitya and the brilliant management graduate Aditya are unable to meet despite several trials.

Arathi, Nitya's daughter is gifted.

Misha, daughter of a CEO of a reputable organization in Mumbai, is a junior in the management institute and a good singer. She falls in love with Aditya.

Though Aditya cannot forget Nitya, circumstances force Aditya to marry Misha...They both move to the U.S.

Laxmi and Anand are born there in the U.S.

Laxmi is closer to the father Aditya compared to the ambitious Misha. Laxmi takes every opportunity to visit India with her father.

During one of the visits, Laxmi and Arathi meet not once but twice.

Arathi stumbles upon the fact that Laxmi may be her step-sister.

The story takes a turn from there...

Chapter 1
The Boy; the Girl

What was it that forced him to look at the wee bit of a girl standing in the balcony opposite to his hostel, he was not sure. He was reminded of an English song. Was it the angelic face or the smile in the eyes, he was not sure. But the girl was indeed attractive though she was very lean and didn't have an attractive figure. Her eyes met his and she turned away.

Aditya had just started his pre-final year of engineering and had another four semesters to complete his engineering course. He was doing quite well in his studies and was known for his oratory skills. He was tall, had a charming personality and was also a good athlete. From a farming family, his father had done well to give the children a good life. His mother was a teacher and she worked not for her salary but because she was passionate about it. She was known for her good teaching skills as well as her dance choreography skills. Aditya had two younger sisters. Both of them were good dancers and also, like him, good at their studies.

He was still watching her when a lady, possibly her mother, came into their balcony. They left together. But before she did, she turned and their eyes met once again.

Consumed by his working days, Aditya didn't think of the girl the entire week except when Sunday came around. He was standing in his room near the window after lunch when he saw her again. She was looking at the hostel. He went out to his balcony. This time there was a flicker of a smile on her face. She was standing in a building which was only nearing completion and no one had moved in yet. Aditya wondered who she was and why was she there on the weekends. While he pondered over this, someone called her and off she went.

He decided to wait till the next weekend to find answers, so when his friends called him to go out to a movie premiere the afternoon of that weekend, he politely declined much to their surprise. Instead, he decided to walk down and go explore the new building. He didn't find anyone at the entrance. So he casually walked up the staircase to the second floor, where he saw her sitting on the floor, reading. Maybe the girl belonged to one of the worker's family, he thought. On seeing him, she jumped up. She seemed a little tense so he told her that he was a student at the engineering college and there was no need to worry as he was leaving.

"I didn't ask you to go. I was shocked, that's all. No one comes here other than my mother and I. The caretaker asked my mother to clean the building once in a week. So when she comes, I come since she is alone. I just sit here and do my school work while she works."

He was a little hesitant to stay. His visit could start rumors. All it would take was one of his friends seeing him with the girl.

"Where are you studying?" he asked.

"HCC," she replied.

"What class?"

"I just finished my 10th grade. Waiting for my results. Should be out in a couple of days."

"How did you do?"

"Quite well." She continued calmly, "I plan on pursuing the commerce stream."

"Well, good luck to you," said Aditya. As he shifted to make a move on, he asked, "By the way, what's your name? My name is Aditya."

"Nitya," she replied smilingly as Aditya started to make his way down the stairs.

******

A couple of days later while Aditya was in the library and going through the newspaper, he was pleasantly surprised. There she was. Her photo under the headline which read 'HCC girl tops Grade X exams'. They had written about her, about how she belonged to the lower strata of the society and yet without the means of modern facilities, this girl had excelled in her exams due to her sheer hard work and her mother's encouragement. The article also mentioned how her father had passed away a couple of months before the exams and besides being the school champion, she was also a very good sprinter, winning several accolades at various competitions. Aditya was thoroughly impressed and he wanted to see her again. *The weekend*, he thought.

Saturday morning, a call from the reception took him by surprise. They informed him that there were two ladies waiting for him. He went down to see Nitya and the lady from the balcony. Nitya introduced her as her mother.

The lady said to him, "I don't know you, but Nitya said she had met you and felt that you were the best person to get some guidance. We do not know anyone like you. As you know, we are daily wage workers. She stood first in the examination and all our friends, even the tutorial colleges, are asking her to pursue the science stream and do medical entrance exam coaching. But she…" looking at Nitya, "is not listening." She looked back at Aditya enquiringly.

Aditya was taken aback as well as a little embarrassed, knowing that quite a few of his friends were watching him. Aditya was generally shy around girls and women, and he knew this little spectacle was definitely generating some curiosity among his friends.

"All of these tutorial colleges want publicity, so they push to get her enrolled in their colleges. Forget them. I read in the newspaper that Nitya is very good at her studies as well as in sports. So if she pursues the commerce stream, she will most probably top in that too as she did now. That will give her a chance to secure a scholarship and complete her graduation and while doing her graduation, maybe she can even take up coaching for the administrative services examination." Aditya continued, "She can join a library and start reading different books. The college near your locality is known to be very good for Commerce." Aditya paused and then added, "This is just my opinion."

"Will she get a scholarship in that college?" asked the mother as soon as he was finished talking.

"I think the college will be more than happy to enroll her since she is a topper. I am sure they will be able to provide her a scholarship."

"But we do not know anyone in that college. And it is a Christian college," the mother said, a little worried.

"Let me see what I can do. Tomorrow." With that, Aditya sent them on their way.

******

On Sunday, Aditya walked to the church on the beach. He waited patiently for the crowd of people to leave the church before he entered. The Father was a friendly person and on seeing a young man in jeans and a T-shirt, unlike the normal congregation of fisher folk, he came forward and said to Aditya, "You don't seem to be from these parts, young man. Where are you from and what can I do for you?"

"Father, I am from a village from the north of the state and I am a student at the engineering college. I came to meet you and ask you for a favor."

"Tell me."

"I need admission for a girl who cannot afford to pay the fee to the college that is connected to this church."

"The college management is different, young man, and it may be very difficult for me to secure admission for you. There is immense pull and pressure for each and every seat. And if she cannot pay the fee then it an uphill task for me."

Father squeezed Aditya's hand and began to turn away when Aditya said, "Even if she is the topper in the state for the grade ten exams?"

Father turned back with a smile, waiting to hear more.

"Nitya…the girl, she is the state topper and…she is from this village. I suggested she take admission in this college for commerce. And that is the reason I am here. I do not know anyone in the college. And the girl and her mother won't even be able to enter the college, let alone get an application for the admission."

The Father paused before he spoke. "Meet me tomorrow early morning before Mass with her mark sheets and the girl of course. What is your name, young man?"

"Aditya."

"And why are you so interested in this girl's admission, Aditya?"

"Let's just say…philanthropy," Aditya smiled and replied.

The Father laughed aloud and said, "OK, see you tomorrow then."

******

Aditya walked back to the hostel. He wondered how to get in touch with Nitya and her mother. After a late lunch, he walked to the building in hopes that he might find them there, being a Sunday. He asked the caretaker when he got there about the lady.

"You mean Santhamma?" replied the caretaker. "She isn't here but she might come. I don't know. She was talking about her daughter and some college. You can sit here. If she comes, it would be within the hour. If not, she might not come today."

Aditya saw some magazines, started to peruse through them and fell asleep in the process.

He woke up with a start. Nitya was towering over him.

"Why do you sleep here and not in your room?" she asked with a smile.

Aditya smiled back, "I was waiting for your mother." He went on to tell her about the conversation he had with the Father and Nitya's face lit up.

"Thank you so much. I will be there early morning with Amma."

"Meet me at the church." He smiled at her and made his way back to the hostel.

******

The Father could not hide his admiration when he saw a newspaper cutting Nitya brought with her. Armed with print outs of her mark sheets and the cuttings, he took them to the college. The lobby was crowded with students and parents, the latter complaining about how they could not get the application form though they had come early in the morning. The attendant was constantly informing the crowd that the forms were all exhausted and they should all leave. There was no point in waiting.

On hearing this, Nitya became nervous and Aditya told her not to worry as the Father had her papers. "Nitya Santhamma" the intercom system announced. Aditya pushed forward and made way for Nitya to reach the office. She was taken inside by the office assistant. It was nearly half an hour before she came out. She was smiling. Father had also a smile. They all walked towards the exit.

"My philanthropic friend, your work is done," the Father told Aditya with a smile when they came out of the college. "She also has a scholarship which will see her through if she keeps up her good performance."

Her mother who was waiting outside could not believe that her daughter had been admitted to a prestigious college on scholarship.

"We have a small house given by the government. If you come, I will give you some tea and something to eat," she said with gratitude. She continued, "We have been waiting from morning and you must be tired and hungry."

"Today is a working day and I am already late to college. Let me run. I will come some other day," said Aditya whilst signaling to an auto rickshaw. He jumped in and they sped away.

******

It was more than three weeks before Aditya had any time on his hands. That Sunday, he went for an early breakfast and later ventured into the colony where the government had given houses for the fisher folk and people that belonged to other backward classes. He didn't know where Nitya and her mother lived but decided to try his luck as he did have their names. There wasn't much difficulty finding them as Nitya was a mini celebrity now in her locality.

Aditya's bike was mobbed by children running after it as he made his way to Nitya's home. The door was open and hearing the commotion, Nitya came out, wearing a lungi and a t-shirt. When she saw Aditya, she was shocked and ran inside. Aditya parked the bike which he had borrowed from his friend and Nitya's mother came out, held his hand and took him inside.

A couple of plastic chairs, a small table, a bed and an almirah were all the furniture inside the house. He sat on a chair close to the table. He saw quite a few books on the table. He guessed that Nitya might have had been studying.

"I did not think you would ever come here. So happy you came." Nitya said to Aditya. She had changed into a long skirt and blouse. She began telling him all about the college and how she had been doing in her classes and in sports. "I have also joined the college choir team," she said with a smile. "The nun who is training us told me I had a good voice."

Aditya had tea, tapioca and a fish cake. An hour later, he made his way to the door to leave.

"When will you come again?" Nitya asked.

"I think it's better if you came to the apartment building on Sunday."

"I will try."

******

Chapter 2
College and Love

It was a Sunday morning. Aditya was getting ready to leave for the cricket game. His college team was not playing this game. Next week, they were playing one of the teams from this game and he wanted to watch the bowlers of that team to help prepare him for his game next week. He was outside waiting for his friend when he saw Nitya waving at him from a balcony in the opposite building. When his friend arrived, he asked him to carry on, saying he wasn't feeling very well. The surprised friend went off after seeing Aditya go back to his room. Aditya waited for a few minutes and then went back down, heading to the apartment building.

"Sorry. I thought you were free…if you have some work, you can go and I will come some other time."

"I was just going to watch a game of cricket. Nothing special. How are you? You look great!"

"Actually, a lot has been happening," she said with excitement. "Seeing my height, the basketball coach asked me to come and try my hand at the game. Last week, I was shown how to play and it turns out, I am good at it. So I was asked to go in every morning, early, for an hour of coaching! Nowadays, I wake up very early to finish my studies and get to college for practice. Oh! And I did not have the proper clothes for basketball, so they have given me a t-shirt, shorts and a good pair of shoes to play in."

Aditya smiled and said, "You must be really good for them to give you all that. I am so happy for you. But please don't forget to focus on your studies also. I play cricket. I am doing quite well in that area and I might get the district selection. But with most of the Sundays spent on the field, it's hard to keep up with my studies. And I have to prepare for my MBA entrance exams next year."

By now, they were sitting next to each other on the floor and Aditya held her hand. She looked into his eyes and smiled. The lyrics of the old country song came to him again…"She had the face of an angel, eyes of an innocent child."

Nitya pulled back her hand and said, "What happened to you? You seem to be far away."

"Nothing…you are very beautiful."

Nitya smiled, which made her look even more appealing to Aditya.

"Amma must be waiting." She got up to leave. "When you get time, please come home."

"One of the days I want to take you to a cricket game and show how the game is played. By the way, our college women's basketball team is one of the best," Aditya said, shaking her hand before she left.

******

Sport, exams and other activities took up most of their time and before they knew it, it was the end of the term when Aditya decided to go and visit Nitya. He was leaving for home the next day. So he borrowed as usual the bike and headed to the colony. Nitya's mother was talking with a few ladies outside her home when she saw him approaching. She quietly went inside. When Aditya saw Nitya, he could tell that she had been sleeping.

"She came very late last evening. She had gone to some college to play," her mother said. Aditya sat with her, while Nitya changed and freshened up. When Nitya joined them, her mother got up and went to make a cup of tea for Aditya.

Nitya then went on to give Aditya a detailed account of events that took place at her college. She was among the top rankers in the college and as far as basketball was concerned, she was playing really well and was now a part of the college team. She had stopped singing to concentrate on her studies and basketball. She was also representing the college in debates. During the short vacation that was coming up, she told him she was planning to do a course in spoken English to improve her language. Aditya was very impressed. She then told him how she was planning to come down to the college hostel to meet him and that's when he told her about his trip back home. He would be gone for ten days. Aditya thought that Nitya's eyes were tearing up. It lasted a moment before she went on to ask him about the trip, his home and parents. He left an hour later but when they said their goodbyes, he felt that Nitya's eyes were moist once more.

******

While having breakfast at home with his father and mother, Aditya said, "Amma, I met an interesting family near my college…only mother and daughter. They are a poor family from the fishing community…very accidental meeting. Anyway, the girl got the first rank for the SSLC exam and I helped her get admission into a good college."

Aditya went ahead and told them the story about getting Nitya the admission when his father interrupted him.

"Is she good-looking?" he said with a smile on his face.

"Just a simple, tall girl…nothing extraordinary. And…she is a basketball player," Aditya replied.

"I am happy you helped the girl and next time when I am down to visit you, you must introduce me to the girl and her mother," said Aditya's mother. Aditya agreed and the conversation moved on to his college, studies, and other things.

******

"Nitya, why are you not chirping around the house like your usual self? Are you upset with something? Or is it because your friend has gone away?" The mother continued to clean the house while she looked at Nitya for answers.

"To tell you the truth, I am a little sad that Aditya is not in town."

"Nitya, you know he will soon be going away for good. He is going to be an engineer and he hails from a rich family."

"I know, Amma, but something inside me tells me that Aditya is different. I don't know how to explain it so let us just wait and see."

The mother shrugged her shoulders. "You are only turning eighteen. You have to make something of yourself to sustain us both. So please think about that," she said that and went about her cleaning.

******

Aditya was standing in his college lobby when he heard an announcement about a women's basketball game. It was his college playing a game against Nitya's college. The game was that Friday so Aditya decided to skip his afternoon class on the day to watch the game. Nitya hadn't mentioned the game to him as she was not aware of the fact that the match was being played at the engineering college. So she was surprised and a little bit embarrassed when Aditya showed up during her break. It had been difficult for Aditya to convince the PE teacher of Nitya's team that she was his friend and managed to raise quite a few eyebrows when he spoke with Nitya eventually.

"You're playing really well and I'm so happy to see you in the team jersey."

Nitya was a little shy and didn't say much but as he was leaving she said, "You have given me all the motivation I need to do better," and smiled.

At the half way point, Aditya's college was in the lead. But when the play commenced after the break, Nitya who was in great form, reduced the lead to just 2 points before the last minute. Nitya then received a pass and in a split second, she jumped, tried a long throw and it went in! Nitya had done it! There was a collective shock all around as the zonal champions were beaten for the first time in almost a year.

Nitya's PE teacher and team mates carried her off the court and she could not see Aditya as they rushed back to the college soon after.

******

The year went by quickly and Nitya's first year of college and Aditya's pre final year were soon coming to an end. Both of them had done exceptionally well, especially Nitya. Nitya got the second rank in her class and she was selected to represent her zone in basketball. She declined to travel as she wanted to concentrate on studies. She only played when the games were in or close to the city just so she could return home every evening. She was also doing well in her debates now, especially after her spoken English classes. As for Aditya, he was judged the best batsman in the district and was called for University selection. He was also engaged in preparations for his MBA examination in the coming year.

******

Aditya was leaving for his study trip. Fifteen days spent visiting interesting places to enhance his practical knowledge in engineering. The exams had just gotten over and at the end of the study trip, students would be leaving for their holidays for about three weeks. Nitya didn't have much to do during her holidays, so when Aditya met Nitya, he had a plan for her.

"Nitya, during your holidays, would you consider doing something new that will also help keep you fit?" he asked with a smile. "I have made all the arrangements. You only have to get up early and take the first bus to the city…"

"My God, Aditya. I really need the holiday after this hectic year. I thought of going to the library and also helping Amma do up our home a little. I have got some money saved from my scholarship…but tell me what do you have in mind?"

"You can still do those things but from 7:00 a.m. to 8:30 a.m., you will go for swimming classes. Here is your swim suit, bag and the receipt for your classes," he said, handing her the things. "It's just four days a week for a month."

"Aditya, you are crazy. I can't go for swimming! People will laugh. I know a bit that is enough."

"You will know the benefits after a month. Apart from the fact that it's fitness training, your studies will also improve. Trust me. Do it for me."

Aditya spoke to her mother as well, who was reluctant at first, but convinced later when Aditya said that she would leave before the village woke up and be back home by 9:30 am.

When Nitya's mother went out to get something, Aditya hugged Nitya and headed out. Nitya wanted to hold him back, instead. With her eyes full of tears, she walked to the door to watch Aditya leaving on his bike.

******

Aditya and Nitya saw each other frequently but only during weekends and for short amounts of time. For Nitya's mother, Aditya was turning out to be good support. She also liked him very much because he was quite the aristocrat in her eyes, never doing anything or saying anything that wasn't proper. She was very aware of how they were placed in the social strata even though Nitya adored him. She didn't understand quite why Aditya was going out of his way to help Nitya; indirectly she too was benefitting from this. Over the past year, Nitya's scholarship and timely help from Aditya made sure she didn't have to do the menial jobs she did in the past. She had managed to get a job tending to the garden at the church, keeping her occupied and earning her a decent amount of money.

Nitya continued to excel in school and after many discussions with Aditya, she had decided to take up Economics for her graduation. At a later point, she would also try out for IAS. Once her mind was set, she concentrated on getting a scholarship to one of the top colleges for her further

20

studies. She was also more conscious of her figure now and paid more attention to grooming and keeping herself fit.

Besides being selected for the university cricket team, Aditya had made it through the entrance examination for his MBA to one of India's premier institutions. He was a fair and handsome young man with intense eyes. Now sprouting a thick moustache, he had quite a few girls after him. He managed to keep them at bay and by now, his fondness for Nitya was quite obvious to his close friends.

Nitya's mother was upset that Aditya was to leave soon. She thought that if this was affecting her so much, she couldn't imagine what was going through her daughter's mind. Right now though, the year end was drawing to a close and both Aditya and Nitya were engrossed in their studies.

It was the day before the last exam which signaled the end of the term. Nitya put down the book she was reading and sat up on the bed.

"Amma," she said looking at her mother, "I want to tell you something. I know you will not like it but I am in love with Aditya. I know it may look foolish to you but to me, it's not. He is everything that I want. He is intelligent, smart, good-looking and, above all, the owner of a kind and loving heart. He didn't need to do anything for us, Amma. Even though there are many rich and beautiful girls pursuing him, it was me…and you, he wanted to take care of. He is leaving the day after and I am going to spend the day with him. I may be foolish and a little crazy and I honestly don't know what is going to happen. But Amma, I am responsible for my actions and you need not worry. I will make something of myself. We will see what the future has in store for us." She smiled at her mother's perplexed face.

"I will leave it to God." That was all the reply she got.

******

Nitya's exams were finally done with. Aditya's last exam was over the previous day and he was gathering his belongings to start packing. He was leaving the next day. He wanted to finish everything by the afternoon so he could spend his last evening with Nitya.

Around five in the evening, Aditya got a call from the caretaker saying Nitya was waiting downstairs for him. Pleasantly surprised, he went down to see her standing there with a couple of bags.

"You are leaving tomorrow and I just wanted to be with you for some time," she said looking at him. "I was not doing anything…I can help you pack."

He was happy to see her but he didn't want to stand there and talk. He thought, with her help he could finish packing quickly and head to her house, so he took her up to his room. Once inside, she said, "I brought you some food so you don't have to go out and eat. Your mess is closed, I know."

Aditya realized that Nitya had other plans and started to get a little nervous. "What is on your mind, Nitya?"

"I want to spend whatever time we have, with you, even if that means I've to spend the night with you. I don't care…from tomorrow I won't be stepping foot into this college…ever."

He sat her down on the bed while he sat on the only chair and started to pack his bag. After a few minutes, she rose from the bed, walked to the door and locked it. She then walked over to the back of his chair, reached out from behind by putting her arms around his neck and caressing his cheeks with her cheeks. Aditya's mind and heart were racing. He was sad and lost that he was leaving her yet he didn't want to do anything that could hurt her in anyway. But he knew he couldn't hold out much longer, his self-control was slipping. He sat frozen while she held him. Nitya thought that when she put her arms around him, he would move away and lecture her for being reckless. But when he didn't move, she was emboldened enough to come around and sit down on his lap. She put her arms around him once again drawing his face to hers. Looking straight into his eyes, she whispered, "I am not going home tonight."

******

It was four in the morning when Aditya woke up. He then got Nitya up, dressed and went downstairs to catch the first bus at five to the colony. There was no conversation. As he walked her home, he said, "I am sorry for what happened last night. I should have had more sense." He stopped walking and looked her in the eyes and said, "If anything happens…please let me know. A child should have a father and I will be there. This is my promise."

They reached the outside of her house and before heading back, Aditya hugged her tightly and said, "I love you and you will be my only love." He knew she was going to break down and cry so he left without turning back.

Nitya knocked on the door and when it opened, she rushed in and threw herself on the bed, letting her tears finally fall.

******

"Amma, Aditya is leaving on the 10:00 a.m. train. Let us go to the station, please. I don't know when I will see him next. There is a 9 o'clock bus to the station."

Nitya's mother had not asked her daughter anything about last evening. She knew her daughter would open up and reveal all when she wanted to. Nitya had slept only for an hour and taken a bath while she was preparing breakfast. The mother agreed and they went to the station.

Aditya was standing on the platform with a couple of friends when he saw Nitya and her mother approaching him. His friends moved away, giving them space to talk. When Aditya reached down and touched the feet of Nitya's mother, Nitya was shocked. He then proceeded to give her mother a hug.

"I have two mothers, one here and one in my village. Thank you for all the good food and good times you gave me over the last two years. I am your son and you can call me anytime…for any assistance. I will be there for Nitya if she ever needs me. I am not going to leave her."

Nitya's mother had tears in her eyes and this time, she pulled Aditya to herself, hugging him and saying thank you. The train was about to leave. Nitya was holding onto him, not letting him go.

"Nitya, I am yours…please keep in touch." He slowly pried her fingers away and walked towards the train.

******

24

Chapter 3
College and the Baby

"Amma, I think we should move from here. I want to go somewhere where we won't know too many people. I will find a good college there and Aditya has given me some money with which we can find a good house to live in. I can give tuitions and with the money I get from the scholarship, I can manage our expenses. I do not know about the future but I can assure you, I will make something of myself." Nitya looked at her mom who was lying by her side on the bed. Almost as if she could read her mother's mind, she said, "Last night, I did something I shouldn't have. You know I have been in love with Aditya for the past two years. Amma, Aditya has always been very good to me and has never stepped out of bounds with me. What happened yesterday was completely on me. So…if something were to happen, I don't want you to have to be here, dealing with these colony people." She continued after a slight pause, "Sorry Amma…forgive me. But please don't worry; everything is going to be just fine." They lay there in the dark, in silence, before drifting off to sleep eventually.

******

As expected, Nitya was the topper in her grade twelve examinations as well. Having stood first in both tenth and twelfth grade in the state, she was bombarded with scholarship offers from various colleges, some adding more incentives along with their offers. She remembered Aditya telling her that 'Economics' was the future so she looked for a good college which had an excellent program in Economics. Her search landed her on a not so prominent college, set in the heart of lush greenery and armed with a library with an expansive collection of books. The college principal couldn't believe his good fortune when Nitya asked to join the institution, and so when she told him that she needed to find accommodation near the college for herself and her mom, he readily obliged by finding a flat almost immediately. The flat was a small one on the first floor of a two-story building and fit within her budget. She paid rent for the first six months and moved in. She had a fortnight to settle in before her classes commenced.

With the money Aditya gave her, Nitya moved their limited belongings into the freshly painted new home, which overlooked a rubber tree estate. Two lady teachers of a school nearby occupied the apartment on the floor above them and the ground floor apartment was where the owner of the building, with his wife and two young children, lived. The owner was proud to have a top-ranking student staying in his building and happy that his kids could have in Nitya a good role model.

For reasons only known to her, Nitya told her neighbors that she was married and that her husband was abroad, studying for his PhD. Though they were a little surprised that such a young girl should be married, they put it down to the norm which existed within the lower strata of society. Even though her mother was shocked the most at her daughter's elaborate story, she didn't let it show, knowing fully well that Nitya had her reasons.

While in college, Nitya steered clear of basketball. The college didn't have great facilities or a good team and she knew that if she did get pregnant, she would have had to stop playing anyway. She opted for badminton instead, just to keep fit and stay healthy. A lecturer encouraged her to join a public speaking club he had recently started up. Nitya joined knowing the skills she would gain from it could help her with her career ambitions.

******

One morning, Nitya's mother gathered the newspaper from below the gate where it was dropped and began perusing through it right there. Nitya had subscribed to the English newspaper. Though her mother could not really read it, she looked at the photographs and tried in vain to read the headlines. Just at that time, the landlord came out to go to his store. He owned a small store nearby.

"Do you know how to read English?" he asked her.

She smiled, neither confirming, nor denying.

"Can you come to my store around 10 o'clock? I want to talk to you." Saying this, he made his way to the store.

When she told Nitya what happened, Nitya laughed and said "Amma, you go and see what he wants. Maybe he needs some help. As long as it does not involve reading or writing in English, I think you should take it. That is if he offers you a job. Even if he doesn't pay well, at least the job will keep you occupied and the money will always come to use. So go and let us see what happens."

Her mother was hesitant even though she knew she had nothing to lose. But at ten a.m., she was there in his shop. The landlord was happy to see her as she was neatly dressed and had a smile on her face.

"I need someone to keep stock of the materials coming in and let me know when I should order for more materials. We often run out of stock because I don't order it on time. If you help me, I can pay you and this can cover your rent…you might still have some extra to keep…So what do you say?"

"I will discuss it with Nitya and let you know the day after. Is that alright?"

She thanked the landlord when he agreed and left the shop. She was going to take the job but she didn't answer immediately because she didn't want to seem too eager. Nitya was happy on hearing the news and asked her to do it but only on the condition that she could be back home by four in the evening. The landlord was more than willing to abide by her terms. He was happy that there finally was someone handling this important aspect of his business. Nitya's mother started working from the very next week itself.

Before she went to work, Nitya made sure her mother knew a little bit about how to take stock of materials. She used her accounting knowledge to create a few formats that helped her mother handle the situations at her new job. She also asked her mother to use her experience from the time she was a cleaning lady as well as take stock of all the materials that were in the store and make a list in the first week itself. With Nitya's help, her mother gained confidence day by day, and the landlord was happy to see that not only was she doing what he asked of her, but also that his shop was always neat and in top shape. He was glad that he had hired the right person for the job.

******

"My father passed away in a fishing boat accident. My mother had to work as a cleaning lady to make ends meet. I knew the only way to survive was to study hard. I did exactly that and stood first in the state for both grade ten and twelve examinations. Now with the money from my scholarship and the tuition classes I give, we are able to sustain ourselves."

"My name is Nitya and this is my story. My life took a turn for the better with the timely arrival of a good Samaritan. He was an engineering student and he encouraged me, guided me and helped both my mom and I…"

This was Nitya's icebreaker speech for her first public speaking meeting. She continued to speak to the rapt audience of twenty-five members and when she was done, she was given a standing ovation. She was careful to avoid revealing too much information about Aditya and herself and only spoke what she thought they needed to hear.

Nitya was doing well in college and she made full use of her college library whenever she got a moment to spare. She learned the college was the brain child of an NRI philanthropist who worked very hard to maintain high academic standards for the college. Even though the facilities weren't too many, he made sure to hire the right people for the right jobs to ensure that the students that graduated from his college were armed with the right skills. The first graduating batch had just completed their exams and with great excitement and trepidation, they waited for their results.

Nitya was sure she was pregnant. She had missed her period. She waited and as luck would have it, it was around this time when the teachers upstairs moved out and a lady doctor and her family moved in. The doctor worked at a local hospital near the college and had a young son who was in a primary class. Her husband was a professor in a medical college in another city and only came home on the weekends. Within no time at all, the doctor and Nitya had become friends.

The results of the college examination, though delayed, were finally out and the students had fared very well with quite a few of them scoring highly. Although the college didn't feature in the top with their results, it received positive remarks from the media. Nitya was glad and saw an opportunity. She had her mind set on taking the college to the top with her results in the coming year.

The landlord had increased Nitya's mother's salary owing to the exceptional work she was doing at his store. On one occasion, she asked the owner to consider opening a small cafeteria because people had to travel quite a while to reach an eatery of any kind. The landlord asked her to look into procurement of small bites from a bakery at a discount so as to make it worthwhile for his business. So she went with Nitya to different bakeries and did the needful. Soon, in a corner of the shop, they set up a cooler to keep all the snacks and a kettle to make coffee and tea.

Although the store did not make a substantial amount of income in the first few weeks, people soon started to come in in large numbers. So they had to get a new freezer and also a couple of tables and chairs to keep up with the demands of the customers. Within a couple of months, the landlord had added an extension to the shop and made Nitya's mother the manager of the cafeteria.

******

Time was passing quickly and Nitya asked her mother one morning to take her to the doctor. Her mother decided to consult the doctor upstairs first. She explained the situation and the lady doctor took Nitya with her to the hospital in her car. There, Nitya's pregnancy was confirmed. The doctor asked her whether she wanted to have an abortion as it was still early. She could help her without any complications. The doctor thought that she was too young and too good a student to have this baby turn her world upside down. It would be too hard for her, especially with Nitya's husband away. But Nitya's mind was made. She was having this child.

"Doctor, I want this baby. This is a baby born out of love and I need the baby for the both of us." Nitya thought of Aditya. Her heart ached and she paused for a moment. She quickly regained her composure and said, "If you would open a file now itself, both of us will really appreciate it. I can give you all the details."

The same day, the file was opened in the hospital with the child's father's name listed as Aditya Pillai.

Nitya and her mom visited all the nearby temples, doing offerings to thank the Gods for their little blessing.

******

The owner of Nitya's college, the NRI Mr. Nair, was going through the new admission register when he came across the Nitya's name marked in it with a couple of stars. On checking with the registrar, he was briefed about her. He wanted to meet with her personally. He checked on her with her teachers and judged by her activities that she was an all-rounder. He hoped that he could motivate her further on meeting with her...maybe she would bring his college the glory he thought it deserved.

While visiting the hospital one day, he saw Nitya and her mother walking out of a doctor's office. Even though he hadn't met her yet, he was sure that the girl was Nitya. He walked into the doctor's office, introduced himself and asked her whether the girl was indeed Nitya. This caught the doctor by surprise and she asked him why he wanted to know who the girl was.

"She is an exceptional student. She studies at my college. We have high hopes for her."

"Yes, she is Nitya," the Doctor confirmed.

"Why was she here? Is she alright?"

"She's pregnant."

Taken aback, Mr. Nair walked out of the office without saying another word.

******

Nitya was beginning to find it difficult to hide her pregnancy. So she decided to do something sensible.

"I don't think I'll be able to attend the next semester. My baby is due." Nitya spoke with such clarity and confidence to the Head of the Department, that she herself was amazed at her courage to make that statement.

The Head was shocked and it took him a while to reply.

"You were running around and playing badminton the other day and today…you are having a baby? When did you even get married?" he cried out.

Nitya calmly told him the same story she had told everyone else and left the Head of the Department to process all that information.

The Head reported it to the Principal and enquired whether there was any procedure to be followed. This case was something they had never come across and the Principal said he would check with the university and let him know. Mr. Nair walked in and the Principal informed him about the situation, which he was already aware of.

"She is the future of our college and we should help in any way we can. Let's get her the permission from the university for a semester off. I don't think it should be a problem. And let's wait and see what happens."

Having taken a great load off her mind, Nitya was able to concentrate more on her studies and other college activities. She continued to ace all her exams and assignments and she had become the best speaker of the club. Her end of semester exams were drawing near.

******

Nitya's mother told the landlord that she needed leave for some time and so she would train someone to take her place. The landlord granted her the leave but wanted her to come in, once a week, to check on things, to which she readily agreed. With sufficient income from the shop and the scholarship Nitya was receiving, they were living in peace, but she worried about life after the baby's arrival. She had been saving every extra rupee. With Nitya taking off for a semester and she not working, she knew it was going to be tough on them.

******

On a Sunday, when Nitya and her mother sat talking after breakfast, the doctor walked in unannounced.

"I have some good news for you for you two." She sat down beside them and continued, "Your college owner, Mr. Nair, had come to the hospital. He paid an advance for the hospital expenses towards your delivery."

On hearing the news, both mother and daughter stared at the doctor, shocked.

"Nitya…you must be very important to the college." The doctor smiled when she said this. And when both Nitya and her mother still had nothing to say, she continued, "By the way, I think you have done extremely well in your semester exams…I sensed that from his conversation with me."

The results were not officially declared. So there was no way of knowing the facts. The doctor sat with the flabbergasted duo for some time more and left. As soon as she left, Nitya asked her mother to get ready. They were going to the temple to thank God for his blessings.

******

Two months had passed since the semester exams. Nitya spent her days walking to the college library, reading books and magazines that were related to her choice of subjects and wandering around the grounds in the late evening.

It was the morning of Maha Sivaratri. Nitya felt a little uneasy so she called up the doctor, who took her to the hospital right away. After an examination, she was admitted. She was given a good single room, courtesy of Mr. Nair, and by the evening, Nitya went into labor. Soon a beautiful baby girl was born and she was given the name 'Arathi Pillai'. The day after Arathi had arrived, Nitya's semester exam results were out and she had stood first in the university. A huge bouquet of roses was delivered to her room on behalf of the college.

******

Having had a normal delivery, Nitya was discharged from the hospital within a couple of days. She went home to a grand welcome by the landlord's wife and children. With the help of her neighbors and the doctor upstairs, Nitya and her mother were able to develop a system and handle things very well. Every time she saw Arathi's face, she was reminded of Aditya, and she held out hopes that he would surprise her someday with an unannounced visit.

During one of the doctor's visits to her home, Nitya asked her, "Will I be able to rejoin college in July? By that time Arathi will be five months old…would that be alright?"

"It should not be a problem since your college is nearby. Whenever you have time to spare, you should come home and feed Arathi if you can. Your mother will be able to handle the situation at home, so you need not worry. She might have to take a few months leave once you start college though. Since you are at home now, she could start work and stop in July when you start college. But I suggest you don't leave your daughter with any baby sitter." She added with a smile, "With the grace of God, she is a healthy child and let us keep her that way."

Nitya was happy that the doctor didn't object to her going back to college. So the next day itself, she called up the registrar and informed him that she would be attending college from the next semester.

******

Her classmates visited her once in a while and that way, she was aware of all what was happening in the college. Three months after her delivery, just to keep fit, she started walking to college in the evenings to play badminton.

One day, Nitya's mother asked her whether the three of them could visit Velankanni. Nitya seemed apprehensive, so her mother immediately said, "It's not for Christians only. It's for everyone. They say it's a good place to go offer prayers. Very powerful."

Nitya didn't want to upset her mother. Her mother never asked for anything and Nitya knew how much she had taken on for her sake, without ever questioning her. So she agreed. When she mentioned the trip to the landlord, he said his wife would also accompany them as she too had wanted to visit the place. To make their journey more comfortable, he provided them with his car and a driver.

******

Aditya had a summer internship and so his summer vacation was restricted to two weeks. He went home and decided to go meet Nitya on the weekend. He had missed her and wanted to know how she was doing. On reaching Nitya's colony, Aditya found someone else residing at their place. He asked around and found out that they had moved away. Someone gave him the name of the college she was studying

34

at and he left for the college. Once there, he was told that she had discontinued her studies. That was all the information they provided. He couldn't get any more information and he didn't know how or where to go to find Nitya and her mother. Disappointed and sad, Aditya returned home the same evening. While contemplating the events that happened that day, he knew that there was no way that Nitya wouldn't return to college. She was an ambitious girl. There was something nagging him though. While at the office, when he had enquired about Nitya, someone had mentioned 'the pregnant girl' in passing. He wasn't sure whether he had heard right but he had had this uneasy feeling within ever since. He decided not to dwell on it and made up his mind to return to her college once his internship was over.

******

Nitya and her mother returned after a week. They had had a good trip and had made a few stops along the way. When she went to college one day, she was informed that a young man had come looking for her. On an impulse, she went to her old place. It was there that she got the confirmation she was looking for. It was Aditya who had come looking for her. She wanted to go find him. She thought of visiting his parents' house but wasn't sure what kind of reception to expect for herself and Arathi. So she decided against it. She would wait another year before deciding what to do.

Chapter 4
Nitya and Arathi

Thanks to the doctor and her gracious neighbors, Nitya had no problem rejoining her college the next semester. She continued to excel in her studies and she had become an exceptional public speaker. Time flew by and Arathi was growing up to be a beautiful girl. She had begun speaking much earlier than kids her age. The doctor once made a statement that made Nitya very happy and think of Aditya. She said, "Nitya, Arathi is very intelligent. She might grow up to be smarter than you." Arathi's first birthday came around and it was a quiet one at home with only the three families in attendance.

The doctor, the landlord and his wife loved Nitya. She helped their children with their studies and they did well in school. One day, the landlord said to her, "Nitya, I am planning on buying a new car. If you learn to drive, you can use my old car." He smiled and added, "But you will have to fill the petrol, my dear."

Nitya had never ever thought about learning driving. But this seemed like a great opportunity and she didn't want to miss it. So she started lessons and within six months, she had her license. She had spent quite a bit on her classes, but it was all worth it when the landlord gave her the keys of his old car and asked her to take it for a spin.

******

Nitya had to go to the college library to get some reference books one Saturday and asked the landlord's wife if she could take the car. "The car is yours whenever you need it, Nitya. You don't have to ask. Come, take the key and go," was her reply. Nitya took Arathi with her. They parked outside the college and while walking in, Mr. Nair drove past them into the college. Mr. Nair waited in foyer for Nitya to walk in.

"Good morning, Nitya," Mr. Nair spoke as mother and daughter approached.

"Good morning, Sir." Nitya was holding Arathi in her arms.

"You have a lovely daughter. What's her name?"

"Thank you…Arathi, Sir."

"You are driving now. Very good. You bought a car?"

"No, no. It is not my car. It is my landlord's. He allows me to borrow it when I need it. I took it today because I wanted to bring Arathi with me."

"How old is she?"

"She will be two next month, Sir."

Looking at Arathi, Mr. Nair said, "Wow! You're a big girl now," to which Arathi smiled. He continued now looking at Nitya, "I have recently started a nursery. After she turns two, you can send her there. You don't have to worry about the fee. We will take care of it. You've done a lot for our college. This is the least we can do for you."

Nitya was overwhelmed. She fought back tears at this unexpected gesture of kindness. She also knew never to refuse help if offered. Yes, she had things under control but this offer would definitely help lighten the load on her mother.

"I don't know what to say…Thank you so much, Sir. You are very kind. I will bring Arathi once she is two. Thank you. I just hope I am able to live up to your expectations of me."

"I know you will." Mr. Nair smiled at her and headed to his office.

When she finished collecting her books and headed out of the library, the clerk handed her the nursery's visiting card. Mr. Nair had asked him to give it to Nitya. Nitya returned home excited to give her mother the news, but she was at the shop. Nitya drove over to the shop, updated her mother on what had happened and on their way home, they decided to visit the nursery.

It wasn't far from home. It was small with good facilities. There were three ladies who managed the children, a cleaning lady and a watchman. There were only six other children there when Nitya took Arathi there for her first day. They all seemed to come from affluent families. Nitya was happy that her daughter had the good fortune to attend this particular nursery. She knew her daughter would be looked after. Arathi had no difficulty adjusting to her time in the nursery. The training at the nursery was exceptional and Arathi was already speaking English fluently. She was a very well-mannered little girl.

******

Nitya's final semester had begun. One of her professors suggested that she begin coaching classes for the civil services examination. Nitya decided that she would do that once she had completed her degree and continued to concentrate on her studies. But that didn't stop her from venturing into the library and reading books related to the civil services whenever she got time. All the support from the college, family and friends that Nitya got so she could concentrate on her studies wasn't in vain. Nitya had once again topped in the university for B.Com.

While she was preparing for the civil services examination, the college offered her a job as a teaching assistant. They encouraged her but there was also a lot of pressure for her to do her post-graduation. That would mean that she would have to move to a different place. So she decided to continue with her preparation and work in the college in the meantime. She earned a good salary and the most important part was that she got to spend time with Arathi too.

She took her exams and when the results came, she had done very well as usual. She had a high rank and she decided to take the Indian Audit & Accounts Services. The training for this was in Nagpur. Her mother, the doctor, the landlord and Mr. Nair were all of the opinion that she should go for it. They convinced her that Arathi was going to be fine and she shouldn't worry about her. The training was for eighteen months and Nitya knew that she could come down whenever there were holidays but leaving her child behind was a tough ask of her. But this was a chance for her to have a career for life and provide a good life for her little girl. She convinced herself that time would fly by and she would be with Arathi in no time at all.

The doctor offered to go with Nitya, her mother and Arathi to Nagpur. She knew they had never travelled very far and this was Nagpur. She wanted to make sure that Nitya got settled in and bring back her mother and the baby safely. They reached Nagpur and stayed at a good hotel, courtesy of the doctor. It was a first of many firsts to come for Nitya and her mother. The doctor, mother and Arathi stayed for five days and once Nitya joined the training, they headed back home.

Chapter 5
Aditya

Adi was a little sad that he could not meet Nitya. And the comment about the pregnant girl upset him a little more. He decided to make another visit as soon as the internship was over. After a week he left for Mumbai to take up his internship. Being a good organization, they had their own guest houses. Otherwise it would have had been difficult to find a reasonable accommodation in Mumbai. Adi had asked for 'Operation Research' area for training. He started and got immersed in his training from the beginning. He wanted a good report from the organization.

One day while he was in office, the GM of the organization walked in. He was speaking to the manager and suddenly his eyes fell on Adi. Manager followed his vision. "Sir, this is Aditya who has come from RIM for his summer training." He smiled at Aditya and went on with his conversation with the manager.

Later that day, manager received a call and he went to Aditya. "GM wants you in his office. His office is upstairs." Aditya was a little shaken. He wondered whether it had anything to do with his work. A little nervous, he went to the office. The secretary smiled and said, "Aditya, right? Just a few minutes, GM would see you shortly."

He was looking at the photographs when the secretary called him and ushered him into the GM's office. There was a good-looking girl, but a little tanned. "Hallo, Aditya. You are from the Royal Institute of Management Ranchi, I understand. Are you?"

"Yes, Sir, good afternoon."

"Good afternoon. This is my daughter, Misha. She has just got her confirmation of admission from RIM. So we thought we would get a little more information from you. But first let me know about you."

Adi told them about his home, his college, graduation and a little about life in RIM.

Both of them listened without interruption. Aditya felt as if he was being interviewed!

"I have another meeting in half an hour and it's about 20-minutes' drive. So we will continue our conversation another day. Thank you."

Adi got up. Misha had a smile and she also said 'thank you'.

******

Friday evening he got a call in his office from the Secretary. "GM wants you to have lunch with him on Sunday. A car will pick you up at 10:30 in the morning from the guest house." Adi wondered whether he should have excused himself. But he wanted a good letter from the organization.

Sunday morning he got ready by 10. Wore a jeans and a white T-shirt. By 10:15 the car came. It took more than an hour on a Sunday to reach the house. It was a villa on the side of a lake up in the hills. It was a scenic place, very quiet after the hustle and bustle of the city.

He was greeted by the GM. "Good morning, Aditya. It was good you started early before the holiday traffic."

Both of them walked into a well-kept sitting room. He was also wearing jeans and T-shirt but a black one!

His wife was very fair but short in height, with good features. "My wife, Meenu. You have met Misha. Meera her sister and Manish her brother."

"This is Aditya. He is from RIM where Misha will be joining for her MBA. He is doing his summer internship in our office." He introduced.

"Misha, why don't you get him a cup of hot coffee. There is some time before lunch."

All of them sat down. "How is the institution, Adi. Heard so much about it. How are the placements?"

Adi spoke about the academics, activities, different specialized courses being offered and about the excellent placement with good salaries. He suggested that when they look for filling vacancies, the company could consider RIM. While he was talking, Misha had come in with the coffee and was listening intently.

"Anyway, I was planning to drop Misha to the institute and will take that chance to meet with your officials and will take it from there."

"Where are you from and what are your parents doing?" it was Meenu, Misha's mother.

"Aunty, I am from a small village near Palghat. We are an agricultural family. My father is fully engaged with the farm with its plants, animals, etc. Mother also helps him. I am the only son. By graduation, I am an engineer."

"Do you play football?" the boy was interested to know.

"I do. But I am a cricketer. I played for the university and now I represent the institute."

"Wow!" Manish was thoroughly impressed.

There was silence for a couple of minutes and Misha asked, "Why are you smiling to yourself? Anything interesting."

"Felt like a marriage interview," Aditya said with a smile.

All of them laughed out loud!

Then it was as if the ice was broken and everybody started talking at the same time to Adi.

Aditya liked Misha's mother as being simple and open. Got along well with her. Meera and Manish were chatterboxes. Misha was comparatively quiet. At the head of the table sat Misha's father, while at the opposite end Adi was seated. Close to him on either side was the mother and Manish.

Aditya was really happy that the mother was noticing what he liked and didn't like on the table. Manish was chatting about football and his heroes. Conversation was mostly about politics, company and Manish's football.

"I have told the driver to be ready by 3 so that you can avoid the evening traffic. You chat with the children and I will take a short nap."

It was past 1:30 and Aditya and Manish sat on the dining table itself while the other three were cleaning. Shortly all of them were on the table.

"Meera, are you in school or college?" Adi asked.

"I am a grade XII Science student and my football expert brother in the 8th. You know my quiet sister is a singer. You should make her sing when she come over to your institute."

"Meera is a chatterbox, you asked a question and you are getting a family history," mother cut in with a smile.

"Misha, do you play any instrument or only vocal," Adi asked.

"I play keyboard and I know harmonium from my classical training classes in school," Misha replied.

"Let us play carrom; we have sometime before Aditya leaves." It was Meera.

The sisters were very good; they beat Adi and Manish easily in both games they played before the driver came.

Misha went to call the parents.

"You should come again; we will go for boating in the lake," Meera told him.

"I will try."

"So, when do we see you again, Aditya? Now that you know the place, do drop in when you have time." It was Misha's father this time.

"Yes, Sir," Aditya moved out to the car.

******

It was almost a month since Adi had been to the GM's house when he received a call from him in the office. There was just about ten days for the completion of training. He went up to the office. The door was closed and he read the name 'PRASHANT MENON, GENERAL MANAGER'. The secretary was inside, so he waited. A few minutes later, the secretary came out and he was sent in to the office.

"Good morning, Aditya. I was leaving for about a week and when I am back, you would be ready to leave. Operations Manager has given a good report about your work. I am very happy that you spent your time learning the work. The secretary will give you the letter in a sealed envelope.

"Now I want you to give me your house address as we are going to the Guruvayur temple. Misha wants to visit the temple before she joins RIM. Tell your parents to expect us for a short visit.

"And if not inconvenient, I want you to meet us at the airport when we come down to enroll Misha at RIM. Will let you know the date and time before you leave.

"Good luck and see you soon."

Aditya was happy that he was getting a good report. He shook hands and left.

Later that day, he called up his mother and told her that the GM of the company he was working with and his family might drop in. He would call them up from Guruvayur before coming down, he told his mother. He didn't say anything about his visit. He wanted to know what his mother would say about the family.

Aditya was planning to go down to his place before the institution reopened after vacations. But he had to stay back a couple of days in Mumbai to complete the work and also to collect the payment due from the company for his summer internship. It was a good amount and he sent half the amount to his father and spent some on his clothes. Remaining money he sent to his account. He returned to the institute two days prior to opening. He had a week before the new students' enrollment.

But Aditya could not take rest as he planned! He received the call from Mr. Menon that he was reaching four days early and wanted him to book a good hotel room. Through the institute office he found a good hotel which was a little far from the institute. He met them at the airport and took them to the hotel in the hotel car. As it was a little late in the evening, he told them to take rest and came back.

The next morning, Misha and Mr. Menon came to the institute and went directly to the admissions office and completed all the formalities. Mr. Menon told the office that in case of any emergency or other need regarding Misha, the contact person was Aditya! After that, he called Aditya.

With him they went to the girls hostel and did all the required formalities. Here too Mr. Menon told the caretaker lady that Aditya was the person to be contacted in case of any need regarding Misha! He said Misha would come down to the hostel the next afternoon. Aditya had afternoon class, so he told him to come down to the hotel in the evening.

The previous week as he was leaving Mumbai, his mother had called and told him about the family and how sweet the girl and the mother were. They had tea and spent some time with them. His mother told him that Mr. Menon had told the father that Aditya was smart and hardworking. They spoke about other things and her mother didn't ask him any further questions about the family.

******

Chapter 6
Misha

The classes had started and both Misha and Aditya were busy with their studies. On Sundays, Aditya would be on the field playing cricket and at evenings either football or cricket. He spent quite some time in the library to make up the time lost for sports as he wanted a good rank. Misha initially didn't want to trouble Aditya but off and on she would call Adi for some help or other. It was a holiday and Aditya thought he should take a little time to go and meet Misha. So after breakfast, he called her and asked her to meet him at the library if she was free. Misha was a little surprised but happy. They met at the library when Misha asked whether they could go out for lunch as she wanted a change from the mess food. Though Aditya was not prepared, he agreed and they took an auto and went to a good restaurant where Adi and his cricket friends used to go. Slowly the ice began to melt and conversation touched on various subjects. "I am not a city girl. My father was in Vizag. His factory was quite far from the city and so I had my college studies in a government college away from the city. I completed my exam there and came down to Mumbai though the family had come over quite some time back. I worked very hard and managed to be in the top ranks. Apart from studies I was the winner of quite a few light music competitions in the university."

"Do you sing Hindi songs or English?" Adi was interested.

"I can sing in four languages Hindi, Malayalam, Tamil and Telugu. I have not taken part in an English music competition. But I like country music."

Aditya told her about his engineering college, cricket, football and his ambition to go abroad and be a top executive in an MNC. There was no conversation about Nitya.

By the time they returned after lunch, they were close friends rather than acquaintances. They decided to meet on Saturday afternoon.

******

On Saturday, Adi took Misha where the institute band was practicing. Both were sitting in the auditorium and the band was playing on the stage. They stopped for some time. A guitarist was playing a tune which was an old country music song of Dolly Parton. Misha was singing softly but Adi heard. "John, Misha here sings. She was singing while you were playing. She is a first year student and a friend of mine."

"Hey Misha, come over. Let us try."

She had a husky voice and she sang so well that all the band members came over and sat around them.

A couple of professors who were walking by also came in. It was not always that one could hear country music.

A band member called the lead member and he walked in with a few friends. Misha was introduced by Aditya.

"Let us try a Hindi number. Can you sing the old song?" the lead member asked her.

"I think I can."

This time the whole band came together.

Misha was a hit and everyone congratulated her and asked her to join them the next Saturday.

Aditya was happy that the band felt she was a good singer to be a part of the group.

"You are going to be very popular, not only in RIM but in the city, because our band plays quite often outside for different types of gatherings. So you have to double your efforts to keep up your studies."

"Thank you so much, Aditya. Finally I feel at home."

Aditya walked with her up to the hostel.

On his way back with only his thoughts to keep company, he was thinking about Nitya and comparing her with Misha. Both were outstanding in the studies and had amazing abilities other than studies. Nitya was still a child prone to emotion while Misha was more mature. He was wondering about that one sentence 'the pregnant girl'. He reached his hotel.

As it was a weekend, his roommates had gone to visit his relatives. He was alone and he decided to iron his clothes for the cricket match tomorrow. His mind was in a little confused state. He was thinking about Nitya and he regretted that he didn't get a mobile for her which everyone had. Being in that colony her mother did not want her to have a mobile as most of the people were without that and they could not afford it. He was sure by this time with her scholarship, she would have managed a mobile phone. He decided to call the college and find out whether there was any contact number. He also decided in his mind that he would keep his relation with Misha at the present level, helping her to find her place in the institute.

Life in the institute was moving at a hectic pace. Sports, activities, studies, tests, etc. gave no time for any other diversion.

Misha was doing well in her studies as the assignments and tests showed. And she was becoming quite popular being a band member. Aditya used to meet her mostly on Saturday evenings and occasionally in the library. Semester exams were approaching and Misha told Aditya that she would be concentrating on studies and would miss out on band performances.

"Good decision! You score good marks in the first semester and the professors and the placement office would take notice of you. That will encourage you further and you will find time for both studies and music in the right proportion," Aditya answered.

Misha was happy. "There is going to be a grand FEST happening during the break. You may need to stay back. Better tell your parents early. My parents may come down as they have not come this side till now."

"Oh! I was planning to go to Mumbai for the vacation. If you are staying back, then I have no problem. I will call up my parents today," Misha replied.

******

RIM had invited another reputed management institute from Nagpur for a get together, comprising of competitions and other entertainment activities. It was a five days affair. The institute was all decked up and everyone was running around making the last-minute arrangement.

Misha realized how lucky she was to be told early that she might be needed. The band was performing almost daily for one function or the other. But apart from that she was quite free. Whenever time permitted, she would go to Aditya and assist him in whatever he was doing. He was in charge of sports competitions. With so many games being played like football, cricket, hockey, ladies basketball and tennis, he had his hands full.

Two days prior to the end of the fest, Aditya's parents came in. They arrived late evening by train. Aditya and Misha both had gone to the station and took them to the guest house. Being a long journey, they had a wash and an early dinner. Before leaving, Misha told them, "Uncle, Aditya here will be busy for another two days. I am not, though I have a few things. So I will come down and take you out and show you around, till Aditya gets free. I will come in the morning and meet you. Good night."

She took leave and returned to the hostel. Aditya stayed back with his parents.

Next two days were busy for Aditya as these were the last two days and the results, trophies and certificates had to finalized and arranged. He went in the evening and took them out and left early morning.

Misha's band performances were all in the evening and went on till quite late. But days were comparatively free. The first day she went to them quite early and on the way she got some refreshments from the canteen. She reached before

Aditya left. He had got some bread and fruits. But they had not started. They were quite happy with some proper food, as they were quite hungry in the morning. She went into the kitchen, boiled some water and made coffee. Aditya's parents were quite surprised but happy. Later she took them for a drive around the city and had lunch outside before dropping them back.

"Uncle and aunty, please come tomorrow evening to the institute and listen to some music our band is playing," she told them before leaving. "Anyway, I will come in the morning with some breakfast. Aditya can have the bread if he is leaving early," she smiled and left.

Next day after breakfast she took them to another part of the city and they did some shopping. Later she took them to the institute and showed them around and had a light lunch at the canteen. Aditya was nowhere to be seen! She left them home.

In the evening, she called up Aditya and told him to bring his parents to the hall where the band was playing. Though busy being the last day, he got a friend to drive him to the guest house and brought his parents. While they were getting into the car, his friend said, "Are these your parents? I saw them in the canteen this afternoon with Misha. I thought they were her parents!"

Aditya was surprised and asked, "Amma, you had come to the institute today?"

"Yes, we went around. Misha was trying to call you but your mobile was switched off."

His friend had a smile on his face! They went to the hall and Aditya got them a good place to sit and watch the program.

Both of them were very happy to hear Misha singing and also with the performance of the band.

******

Next day, Aditya was late in getting up after a late night. By the time he woke up his mother had made breakfast. It was simple bread, butter, fruits and coffee. They were sitting having breakfast when his father said, "If your friend Misha was not there, we would have been stuck in the room, don't you think?"

"No, *Acha*, then I would have found some other way. By the way when her father came for admission, I did a lot of running around for them."

"You are a boy and she is a girl," his mother said.

"Amma, she is an MBA student and there is no difference."

"OK, OK, let us leave it but I think when we go out for lunch or dinner, you should invite her."

Later on they went out and Aditya took them to the village nearby where there were lots of handicraft items exhibited in a temple ground. His mother was very interested and bought quite a few items. They then went to a roadside dhaba and had hot chapathi and spicy curries. After lunch they went to a mall and did some more purchases. Coming back they were all tired and went off to sleep. They woke up hearing the call for the prayer from a nearby mosque. After bath, Aditya called Misha and asked her to be ready for going out for dinner.

******

Being a little early the food court in the mall was not crowded. Misha went with Aditya's mother to choose some food. As they returned, Adi and his father got up and went for their choice of food. Both Misha and Adi's mother were vegetarians. When all were having their food, Adi's mother asked, "Misha, why didn't you come home during your holidays? You were there only for an hour when you came down for your temple visit."

"Aunty, I have the summer internship like Adi last year. Because of summer internship, I am sitting with you today! I will try to get an internship in Chennai or Bangalore. If I get it then I can come down during the weekends."

They chatted about this and that and after dinner Adi drove first to the hostel to drop Misha. As she got out, Adi's mother came out of the car along with the father. She hugged Misha and said, "You are such a sweet girl, let us keep in touch."

"Sure, aunty," and she shook hands with Aditya's father and said bye to Adi. Her eyes were moist.

On the drive back, there was no talk in the car.

******

Time does not stop. Days became weeks and weeks into months. Adi did very well in his exams but Misha surprised Adi by being the first rank in her first semester exams. She was very popular with the staff and management as being good in both academics and as a singer. Being a quiet person she was liked even more by everyone. But things were slowly changing. As the second semester was half way, Aditya noticed that Misha was getting a little more authoritative and sometimes stood by her views unlike in the initial days. Aditya started admiring her a little more. Then it was time for placement. Being a cricketer, academically brilliant and a good leader, Adi received quite a number of offers. He didn't take any of them. He was waiting and soon he was offered an international placement in Dubai by an MNC. He decided to take it.

"Will your parents be happy that you are leaving them alone?" Misha asked.

"Misha, they are healthy and not that old. If I go out and earn some good money, I will be able to help them better in days to come. And I don't intend to stay for more than five years. Need some international exposure."

Misha was not convinced but didn't say anything.

By a coincidence, Misha got her summer internship in one of the top textiles mills based in Coimbatore which was only a couple of hours from Aditya's house.

******

Just before the end of session, after the examination, there was a week when students prepared to go in for the summer internship or to take up their new jobs. Few students had asked for a couple of weeks' time before joining the new jobs. Adi decided to go down and look for Nitya. He told Misha that he would just go for four to five days to his home to meet his parents as he would be leaving for Dubai shortly. He told her to wait till he returned before going home on her way to Coimbatore.

With the money he had saved, he took a flight and directly went to the college to look for Nitya.

It was just a quirk of fate that Nitya with her daughter and mother had left the place along with the house owner's family to Mookambika Temple just two days ago. Even the doctor and her children had also accompanied them. Nitya had thought if Adi was to come, he would do so during the holidays which were another two weeks later. She didn't know about his placement and moving off to Dubai. Adi could not get any information and even when he went to the house, there was no one. He was disappointed and sad. He took a taxi back to his house.

At home his mother went on asking about Misha and said, "I really would like a girl like Misha to be my daughter-in-law." She didn't tell Adi to marry her but the undertone was not lost on Adi. But his mindset at that moment was not suited for that discussion and he avoided an answer. He stayed for two days, visited the temple nearby and told his parents that it would be sometime before he could come back and visit them as he was taking up a new job outside the country. His parents didn't show any undue emotions as he left. It made him feel a little more at peace with himself.

******

Adi returned to the institute just the previous day of Misha's departure to Mumbai. As soon as he reached, he called her and they met for lunch at a quiet restaurant outside. She asked about his trip and about his parents. She noticed that he was a little off as his answers were all very short and to the point.

"You seem to be preoccupied, is it anything to do with your parents or your trip to Dubai? If you open up, it will help you. And you know I don't speak to anyone at home or your parents about our conversation. For me you are the ideal I look up to."

Adi was quiet and went on with his food slowly. Misha didn't force him. Anyone looking at them would have thought how two young people could sit so quiet without even looking at each other.

"Misha, will you marry me?"

Misha dropped her spoon on the floor! Her mouth was half open! It took her a full two minutes to recover from the shock of what she heard.

"Adi, you have completely shocked and surprised me. And I am completely lost. So let me sleep over it. I don't want to speak and discuss about it right now."

They both were quiet with their own thoughts. In fact, Adi was happy in his mind that she didn't give an answer right away. His respect for her grew a little more as a person with maturity. He didn't pursue this matter and spoke about his trip and her trip to Mumbai.

Later, he dropped her to the hostel.

******

Misha was packing her things and her mind was racing with many questions. Her friend in the room was going on talking to her but half the time she didn't get any answer and when she would get an answer, it would all be in mono syllables. She had dinner alone in the hostel mess and went to the common room and sat with a magazine. It was quite late when she went to sleep. Her flight was around noon. Adi called her in the morning and told her he would pick her up at 9 and drop her to the airport. In the car she said, "Adi, I have no reason to say no to your proposal as you are my ideal in every way. But I would rather talk to my parents and tell them before I say 'yes' to you. Hope you understand."

"I am happy, you didn't say 'no' to me. I do not mind waiting for the 'yes'," Adi replied with a smile. He took her hand and held it and said, "I will love you with all my heart."

Adi got out of the car and took her bags and walked with her to the counter and just before security, asked her, "Can I give you a parting hug?" She dropped her hand bag to the floor and gave him a real bear hug and touched his cheeks with hers. She picked her hand bag and walked off without turning back. Adi watched for a long time and moved off.

******

Misha made it to Aditya's house twice during the summer internship during weekends. She reached on Saturday mornings and returned on Sunday evenings. Aditya's parents were very happy and made sure her stay was very comfortable. They showed how the work in the farm changed according to the weather. During the times she visited, the weather changed from summer to monsoon. Misha was surprised at the changes the rains brought with the parched ground suddenly turning green and the plants and trees all looking very green and fresh.

During the summer internship, her mentor at the company encouraged her to take up toast master's training. He introduced her to his club and she had her first ice breaker speech in the same club. It was a good speech appreciated by all. This motivated her to continue with it when she returned to the institute.

She took up the toastmasters and moved away from her singing with the band much to the disappointment and heartache of the band members. She spent her weekends preparing speeches. Being good in English, she soon became one of the best speakers of the club. Just before her final semester examinations, there was a national level competition of toast masters at Chennai. Misha was her club's representative.

At the competition there were only four female competitors while there were more than twenty male competitors. After the two rounds, four were selected for the final round. Misha and one more girl were coming there. They had not met as they were in two different segments and two each selected for this from each segment. On the final day when they introduced, Misha came to know the girl was a mother and her name was Nitya. They met at the hall before commencement of the competition. "You look so young to be a mother!"

"I got married at a very young age being the custom in the village," Nitya answered.

"Where is your husband?"

"Oh, he is abroad, studying," Nitya answered.

"What a coincidence, my would-be husband is also abroad!"

At that time there was the announcement for the competition commencement. "Best of luck, Misha," Nitya told her and moved to the front of the hall.

"Thank you, wish you the same."

It was a tough competition but Misha had to admit that Nitya was the best speaker among the four of them and rightfully she won the competition. As Nitya was in a hurry to get back to the college, she came and told bye to Misha and went off.

During the summer internship, Misha had called up Adi after her first visit to his parents. "Adi, I have thought for quite some time and if you still want to marry me, I would be happy to be your wife." They chatted for a few minutes and agreed to meet during the winter break.

Adi would take a couple of days off and fly down to Mumbai.

Misha did extremely well and she waited to get a placement if possible in Dubai but unfortunately she got a good break in Singapore. After discussion with Adi and her parents, she decided to take it up for a year and later try for a move to Dubai.

******

Chapter 7
Nitya

Nitya did very well in her training and she was given a good posting in Vizag. She could have managed a posting in Kerala if she had waited for a couple of months. But she decided to take this up as she wanted a change of scene!

After the training she went home and got everything packed and was ready for leaving. She went to the college and thanked everyone, especially the owner. She was in tears when she sat with the doctor and the house owner. She promised them she would visit them quite often. And with her mother and daughter left for her new place in train as they had quite a bit of luggage. Before leaving, she cleaned up the flat and left the furniture she had purchased.

The gesture was appreciated by the house owner as they could rent it for a higher figure.

Nitya went to a hotel and decided to stay for some time till she could get her apartment allotted. News about her arrival and about her rank had already reached the department head. So when she went to report for her duty, she found everyone good and helpful. Within a week she got her apartment and with help from her office colleagues, she got the necessary furniture. It was an apartment complex and her mother could get to know a few Malayali families within a short time.

Arathi was nearly four and was indeed very smart. She had picked up Hindi and English from the doctor's and house owner's families. She was smarter than a normal three-year-old.

There was a naval school mainly catering for the children of the naval officers. There were a few others, mainly children of government servants and of some local VIPs. Nitya took

Arathi for a test to admit her in KG-I for the forthcoming academic year. They had a couple of tests including a psychometric one. After the test they went home as the results were due after a week. But the next day, Nitya received a call from the school and asked her to meet the Principal along with Arathi. She was a bit worried and tensed. But little she did know that she was in for a great surprise.

Next day, she took half day off from the office and went to the school. The Principal's office was not a large one but a well-kept one. There were three people in the office including a lady. "Mrs. Nitya Menon, you are lucky mother! You have a genius of a daughter in Arathi."

Nitya was shocked and surprised as she had spent less than two years with her daughter with training, college, etc. taking up her time. She couldn't believe her ears. She didn't speak for a few minutes.

"Thank you, Principal Sir," finally she spoke. "I never knew. So what do I do?"

"I will ask our management and regional educational officer whether I could enroll her one class higher!"

"Sir, I would rather she join the class as a normal student and if she is good as you think, you could promote her during the midterm. I would wait till that time for the regular admission though I will pay the fee. You could consider Arathi as a guest student."

"You are very cautious or skeptical, it seems. Anyway, it is not a bad idea. She will get used to the school by that time. Our school uses modern method for studies. So probably it is better she goes a bit slow. Anyway, let us see. You complete the registration formalities and I will keep it pending."

Nitya was very happy. Arathi went on playing with her doll oblivious to all that was happening around her.

Nitya's work took a lot of time away from her. Arathi was on her own for her studies as her grandmother couldn't help much. Nitya during the weekends went through her books and found she was getting all 'stars', gold and red for her work in the class. Occasionally she asked a few questions and Arathi answered while playing. Nitya too realized her daughter was more than gifted. She also realized that she had covered more than half the book in a month. Teachers were giving special attention.

Nitya asked, "Arathi, are you in the same class where we went together the first day?"

"No, Mummy, I sit in a room with lots of computers, TVs and magic boards."

"You play on computers?"

"No, they give me so many drawings and ask me to work on it, the way I like. I do a lot of things on computer. It is really fun!"

Nitya was again surprised.

She didn't even know Arathi could work on a computer!

Six months later just before the closing of school for summer, Nitya went to school to find out about the progress of Arathi. Again Nitya was in for a surprise. As she went in with Arathi, the office receptionist told her that she should meet the Principal. Principal had instructed that whenever Nitya came, she was to be sent to his office. She went to the secretary and told her to inform the Principal that she was in the school. A few minutes later, she was called in.

"I am a little selfish, because I want my school to be in the news. And I will soon project your daughter Arathi. She is not yet five, normally just about to start KG-2, but we are promoting her to grade 1 and possibly by midyear, she would go to grade 2. If she continues here she would probably the youngest child to pass grade 10. Congratulations Mrs. Menon for giving us a child prodigy."

"If my daughter is not unduly stressed and if you provide her all the support, I do not mind."

"I told you I am selfish, so it's in my interest that I help her grow the way she wants so that she enjoys her studies. Do not worry at all."

He gave her a cup of coffee and Arathi an ice cream.

******

A year later while she was still in grade 2, Arathi was trained to appear for an international bench mark test from UK, which was for grade 3 students. She topped not only the school but the whole state and was awarded a certificate as one of the gifted students. With the educational minister's permission, she was promoted to grade 3.

Being a little tall and fair girl, Arathi was not too small for the class. She started to take up tennis lessons in the school.

Arathi did extremely well in school. For her, maths and science were the favourite subjects and she kept on scoring 100% in both the subjects. She was not always the first rank in class as she was not at her best for social science.

A couple of years later, one day Nitya was sitting with Arathi and doing some school work with her.

"Mummy, are you a single mother?"

Nitya was taken aback by that question, "What did you say?"

Arathi repeated that question!

Nitya took a couple of minutes. "I am not going to ask you what prompted this question. But in a strict sense I can't say I am a single mother. This is because, your father came in search of both of us twice. But due to fate or our bad luck, I or both of us were not there at home. I know he came because he went to the college when I was a student. But later when I wanted to look for him, he had left the country. Your father is an engineer from Trivandrum college of Science and Technology and MBA from RIM institute of Management. His name is Aditya Menon. If God's will is that we should be together, one day it will happen. For the time being, I will fight my own life's battle."

"Thank you, Mummy, for your honest answer. I knew a little bit from grandma. And I am proud of you. I would do my best to make you and my father proud of me."

Nitya felt a great burden had been lifted off her back. She knew she would be able to perform better.

Days were passing off quickly. Nitya being sincere and hardworking was always under pressure and as her abilities came to be recognized, her responsibilities grew at times more than she could handle. A lot of travel also added to her schedule. She had no time to think about anything else. On weekends she made sure she was at home with Arathi and her mother. Despite a lot of resistance from her mother, she got a maid to do cleaning and helping at home. That way her mother could spend more time with Arathi. On evenings Arathi used to go for walks only with her grandmother. There were a couple of parks nearby and Arathi enjoyed the greenery, the birds and the breeze from the river nearby which had hardly any water though were very wide.

Arathi on her part was growing up and she was getting taller. Her tennis was also improving and at school she got a good coach who was a state player before. She was a junior champion though she was a sub junior. And by the age 13, she had completed her grade X. She had a special liking for computer science and information technology. She decided to take it up as a career. She topped the school for grade XI and XII and joined a nearby college for BSc data science. She wanted to be a data scientist.

******

There was a feeling among colleagues and friends of Nitya that her husband had left her and most of them felt sad for the family. Nitya though quite good looking had been careful with her dressing. She was always wearing long jacket over her dress which was mostly jeans or pants. She had insisted on Arathi wearing jeans and long shirts or jackets. Her perception was that of trying to be a non-entity. But as she went up the ladder in her work, she had to move to an independent house with a security at the gate and a car with a driver! She had very few friends. Most of the friends were through her mother but all of them were of an older generation. Arathi's few friends used to drop in once in a while.

Arathi, being smart, used to search on web for 'Aditya Menon'. But there were too many. Once or twice she had come across an 'Aditya Menon' who was an engineer and

MBA but he was in the USA. She used to look for 'Aditya Menon' in Dubai but the qualification didn't match.

Little did she know that Aditya was posted by his company in Dubai in New York for a long assignment.

******

Chapter 8
Aditya and Misha

It was the break before the last semester. Misha was supposed to join the Singapore firm within 15 days of taking her final exam. They had asked her to send her passport and other details one month before the end of the session. She decided to keep only the necessary things and carry all the belongings to Mumbai during the trip. Adi was coming down for a couple of days. Rather than a flight, she decided to take the fast train which would take about 22 hours. It was convenient as the train left by 4 in the evening and she would be home by lunch time the next day. Her father met her at the station and on the way had a long discussion on her trip to Singapore and about Aditya, who was coming down the next day evening. She was very tired. After a good bath and some snacks, she went to sleep and got up the next morning. Her mother didn't wake her up as she wanted her to be fresh and happy when Adi come down the next evening.

Misha woke up quite early before everyone. She had a wash and went to the kitchen and made herself a cup of coffee and toasted a couple of slices of bread and buttered heavily and sat down with the newspaper. She also sent a message asking about the flight time to Adi.

Later she went up to her bedroom and started cleaning it up. While she was doing that her mother came in and sat down. "Shall we arrange a small engagement ceremony? It would be difficult after this as you are planning to leave for Singapore and he is in Dubai. I know it is on a very short notice. I do not want to invite a lot of people, just our few relatives here in Mumbai. We will do it on Sunday morning."

"I don't know, Amma. A little too quick, I think. And we haven't spoken to Adi and his parents. His parents should be here."

"Daddy spoke to them yesterday night and has arranged for flight tickets for tomorrow. He has arranged their stay at the company guest house. He also asked Adi's father to speak to Adi today before he flies out."

"So you have already decided. It was only a formality to let me know. Amma suppose I had said 'no', what would have happened. Amma, really, I am not yet ready to decide on a long time commitment. You should have given me time. I pray and hope that both of us are compatible. Like my father, I am really ambitious and I want to be someone on my own merit. Hope you understand. Anyway, for the time I am not standing in your way."

Misha's mother looked at her daughter for some time and slowly left the room. She didn't bring up the subject with anyone, just prayed for Misha and her happiness.

******

As her father was busy, Misha took the car to pick up Adi from the airport along with her mother. Both didn't speak much during the half an hour drive as there was not much traffic. Flight was a little early. So they were just on time. Aditya had a lunch meeting and he had directly gone to the airport from the meeting. He had already packed his bag in the morning and was one of the last passengers to board. So he was in his suit. Tall and fair, he looked really handsome. Misha was the first one to pick him up among the passengers coming out. And she suddenly lost all negative thoughts and really felt a little proud and was happy to welcome him with a hug. Her mother noted the change. Adi bent down and touched the mother's feet and she held his hands and looked at him with eyes brimming with tears of joy. On the way they spoke about his studies, job, institute and about his parents' arrival the next day. Her father had not reached home but both sister and brother were there.

While they were having tea her father joined them. Adi had taken off his jacket and tie but still looked a little too official. "Aditya you seem to be going for a meeting. This is home. Be comfortable. Why didn't you change? You are staying with us tonight. Tomorrow you can move when your parents arrive. Misha, take him to the guest room. Let him have a wash and change his clothes."

"Let him have his tea. Then he can go," the mother said.

Later Misha took him to his room. Her brother accompanied them. "You know, today the national football semi-final is taking place. It will start in 15 minutes. Kerala is playing with Maharashtra. It will be a great game. If you change fast, we can watch together." Misha's brother was holding on to Aditya.

"You start watching. I will join you soon. I want to talk to your sister regarding her job in Singapore for a few minutes, OK."

"You must come soon," he went back.

Misha sat on the bed while Aditya took out his jacket and tie and sat down on the couch.

"I can't understand my parents. They arranged this engagement without asking me," Adi spoke.

"It is not your parents. It is my mother. I also told her she should have waited before fixing the engagement. I have not even settled."

Both of them chatted for some time and Misha left so that Adi could change. Aditya took out his shorts and t-shirt and came out. Misha's brother came running and pulled him to the TV to watch the match. His parents were also there. Only the two sisters were not there.

"After the match, we will have an early dinner," Mr. Menon told Adi. "You must be tired after the flight and your work." Adi just smiled.

At the dinner table, Mr. Menon asked, "Adi, what are your plans and how do you think both you and Misha will be able to work together?"

"Uncle, Misha is an ambitious girl by the look of it and I am also interested in a good career. So we may have to wait a bit to know the exact road ahead. Give us both a little time. I think Misha will agree to that."

"Adi is right, Daddy. I have not even started. It is another four to five months for me to start my career. We will see after a year whether I could move over to Dubai or Adi could move to Singapore. In between, we will travel either way and meet each other."

"Good that both of you have the same thought process. Let it go on like that. Adjustment and little sacrifice are required for a successful life. God bless you both!"

No one else joined in the conversation.

Next day, Adi moved to the guest house with the parents and on Sunday at a private ceremony, the engagement was done. Adi left the same evening. Misha stayed for a week before returning to the institute.

******

Chapter 9
Nitya and Arathi

Life was an express train for Nitya. The more she put an effort to be on top of her work, the more responsibilities were added. She worked late in to the nights. She had to travel quite a bit. Most of the times she had a colleague to travel with her. He was very polite and had a helping nature. Over a period of time, she was depending on him quite a bit. Sometimes she wondered whether she was in love with him. He was from Hyderabad and was a chartered accountant. Slightly older to her she felt but he was of the same rank as she was. Once or twice he had come home when she was late. Arathi spoke to him about tennis and other games. Her mother liked him. One day she asked, "How long are you going to be like this? I may not be there forever and Arathi will one day find a boy and you will be left alone."

"Amma, don't force me. It will happen one day." She thought of her colleague. But she was not sure.

One weekend, Arathi had to go to Hyderabad to play for her school. The school had reached the finals of the interschool championship thanks to the brilliant game being played by Arathi. She was ranked No.1 in the junior section of the state.

Before the game she was sitting in the locker room when the girls from the other school came in. She wished them. And while talking the girl asked, "You are coming from Vizag? My father is there. He is working in the AG's office. It is quite some time since he has come over this side. I don't blame him, because it was a child marriage. He was married to my mother when my mother was only 10 and I think he was 15."

Arathi asked, "What is his name? My mother is there. I will try to find out."

"Kesav Reddy," the girl replied.

Arathi just smiled. While playing she didn't know whether she should throw the game off. She didn't. Though she lost the first game, she played very well and won both the games. She and her team won the trophy and returned.

In the night, Arathi told her mother about the meeting and what happened.

Nitya felt the Almighty was making sure she didn't have to take any decision! But the next day she went to her boss and asked for a change in her portfolio. Though he was surprised, he did do the needful as she was an asset not to be lost. In fact, she decided not to fritter away her energy and concentrate more on her work and Arathi.

******

Arathi was at her best after she left school and started college. She liked the subjects and she did extremely well. Computer Science and Data Science interested her so much. After the first year, she had a short vacation. During the vacation she read about Henry Kissinger the great diplomat of USA. It had an effect on her. She wanted to be a diplomat travelling around the world. She joined an online coaching center for the administrative service examination. And started to read books to enhance her vocabulary and general knowledge. It was as if her life's purpose was to be a foreign service officer. She told her mother what she was doing. Nitya was very proud of her daughter and she encouraged her, though she knew that career would take her daughter away from her. Though she completed her graduation with flying colours, she could not appear for the IAS examination as she was underage. She took up master's course in Data Science while continuing her preparation for the IAS exam. For all the mock exams she scored very high marks. And to polish her speaking, skills she joined British Council training for spoken

English. At the age of 21, she appeared for the exam and was one of the top ranks and took up the IFS training.

******

Arathi took up her tennis again at the training institute. It took only a week for her to get back her rhythm. And she was noticed by all as a good tennis player. It helped her to keep up her good healthy physique as well as a sharp mind. Little did she know at that time that her tennis may become useful one day for a special purpose.

******

Chapter 10
USA

Misha did very well in her semester and she moved to Singapore. A very determined girl, she pushed herself into her routine in right earnest. Within a couple of months she was confirmed in her position which usually took six months. She took up a furnished studio apartment and usually cooked her own food except her lunch. Her apartment also looked almost like an office.

Misha enjoyed her work and she was given more and more challenging assignments. She travelled quite a bit to the neighbouring countries like Malaysia, Indonesia and Vietnam. Around Christmas time, she decided to take a break and go to Dubai for a fortnight to be with Adi. She called up Adi and told him to take a few days off. Adi himself was moving places. Within a year and half, he was the youngest manager in his firm. And it was almost certain that within six months he would have to go to New York for a new assignment. Though he was busy, he also wanted a break and welcomed the idea of having Misha for the Christmas period.

Misha arrived one early morning. They reached Adi's flat around 4:30. Adi told her to take rest for a few hours while he would go to gym and catch up with a few urgent calls from New York. Misha was tired after the long flight and after a wash she decided to have a short nap. It was 9am when she woke up. She freshened up and came down to the dining room where Adi was sitting with a newspaper. Adi gave her a tight hug and moved on to make a cup of coffee. "There are some sandwiches and boiled eggs on the table. And some fruits. No idlis or dosas, sorry!"

Misha just smiled. "How are you and how is your work. Let me hear that first."

While making coffee, Adi in a few short sentences told her about what he was doing and his possible travel to New York.

Ambition was Misha's adrenaline. And when she heard about Adi with her HR background she knew Adi was doing really well. She felt elated and she just moved over to Adi and hugged him and kissed him full on his lips. Adi was pleasantly shocked, "I am so happy for you, Adi. Tonight we are going to the poshest restaurant in town and having a candle light dinner. And I am paying for it!"

Adi took her to his office and introduced to his colleagues. They had a light lunch in the office and then went to one of the well-known malls and bought her few dresses, perfumes and some pearl jewellery. It was late in the evening when they returned to the flat and had little time to wash and dress as they had quite a drive to the restaurant. Shang Palace was a boutique restaurant and frequented by the top business people and film fraternity. They had a corner table.

"I will have cabernet sauvignon," said Misha. That was the best French wine. Adi was a little surprised. He had assumed that Misha didn't drink.

"I will have a beer," he said. It was a lovely dinner. There was music by a favourite pianist. They left quite late.

Adi left his car in the hotel as he did not want to drive after drinks. They book a taxi. Misha went on chatting about the music, food and the service…

They reached home and while Misha was changing her jewellery, Adi went to the bathroom to wash and change. He came out, "Let me just look at the mails while you change," he went down. Misha changed to a sheer voile gown. She felt proud and that her would-be husband was going places. It turned her on…

"Seems you are in a mood to seduce me! Don't you think it's better to wait till we get married," Adi had come up and was smiling.

"I will call Dad tomorrow and tell him to have a registered marriage in a day or two. We will go down tomorrow to Mumbai. You can return immediately," Misha answered while moving and hugging Adi.

"I still think…" Misha didn't allow him to complete his sentence as she kissed him full on his lips…

Misha was in a blissful sleep when Adi got up early and went to his gym. His mind went back in time to his college and hostel and wondered where Nitya was and what had happened to her…

As he came back from the gym, Misha was dressed to go out.

"Where are you going so early in the morning?"

"I had heard first night would be a miserable night. But I got lucky. But I should not push my luck too much. So I need to go to a pharmacy at the earliest! And I have a lot to do before I think of a baby! You know, Adi, ambition and success turn me on and I want to reach some place; where, I am not too sure now but I need to keep up with you. Both of us together will create something…Now tell me where is the nearest pharmacy?"

"It is just next to our building. I will just come down with you." Adi was sweating but it didn't prevent Misha from giving him a hard bear hug.

She went into the pharmacy and got what she wanted. The girl in the pharmacy had a smile as they left!

******

"*Acha*, I think I will be ready for the marriage before April. Please speak to Aditya's parents and do what is required. I have already spoken to Aditya," Misha called up her father in the morning.

"Let us not hurry for a register marriage. But you please be ready. If you go to the States, just make sure to get a few days off for the marriage. In fact, it would be better as we can avoid a lot of family gatherings after marriage!"

Misha was speaking to Adi on the breakfast table.

"I hope you will get your posting after marriage so that I can also accompany you. I will try to get my US visa in Singapore itself."

Adi was thinking of the way Misha was planning her life and future.

"Where are you? You are somewhere else. Did you hear what I said?"

"Of course, Misha, you were saying about getting your visa from Singapore." Adi smiled.

"You get dressed. We will go out and look at all the new shops in the mall which has come up and catch a movie after that."

"Wow, that is really great. I will take only a few minutes," she ran up.

The maid had come. So Adi told her not to prepare any food and just to clean up quickly so that they could leave…

******

Misha could stay hardly for a week as her boss had to leave for an urgent business trip and he wanted her back in the office. But the days were hectic and she really enjoyed her stay both physically and mentally!

As she left, Adi was wondering whether he would be able to come up to her expectations or whether he wanted to come up to her expectations!

******

Aditya decided to join a club as he wanted some physical exercise other than the gym. He was a sportsman at heart and he wanted to play some game. Cricket was difficult with his work and the harsh weather. So he decided to take up tennis as there was a coach at the club for beginners. Three or four times a week he would go to play. Once he got the hang of it, he started playing with his friends from the office whom he took to the club as guests! Mostly they played in the nights.

******

Misha's boss was away for almost a fortnight in the US. He was negotiating for a new contract. One night he called up Misha and asked her to go to the US embassy and apply for a business visa. It took about ten days and she flew to Los Angeles to be with her boss. It was quite an unexpected trip. They both returned in a week. The contract would be signed in Singapore and the work had to start in about three months. Misha was chosen as the leader of the team to get the initial work moving. She had to leave in about four months' time. She called up Adi and gave him the news and added that she was calling up her parents and asking them to get the marriage arranged before she left. She told Adi to inform his parents.

Once again Adi's mind was in confusion. She was very excited to take up her new assignment in Los Angeles, while Adi when he would be posted would be moving to New York. What kind of a relationship it would be with two people almost five or six hours away from each other even by flight!

A couple of days later, Misha called and told him that she was taking up this job to get a foothold in the US and later she would move to New York possibly with another company. Or she would get her present company to sign up a new contract. She was very sure in her mind!

******

Early April, Adi and Misha got married. They could stay only for a week as Misha had to leave for US by the month end. They decided to have their honeymoon in States as they were travelling up and down between the two family houses meeting unavoidable relatives.

******

Misha left for Los Angeles by mid-May and she was fully immersed in her work for almost three months. She liked challenges and especially as she was learning new techniques

74

in HR. She was helping to set up a lean organization recruiting efficient staff. It was a tough job. But her job was being noticed by the client organization. She was doing the HR job for her company to prepare them to take up the contract. And the client company was noticing her efforts. By the year end the client company offered her a position in Chicago and they sweetened it with an offer to apply for her green card! As Misha's company didn't want to offend the client, they didn't object to her leaving.

Meanwhile in Dubai, Adi was offered a better job by another American company. So his plan of leaving for States got delayed. The aircraft company who hired Adi wanted him to join by the New Year. His posting was in Cleveland. When Misha heard about it she was very happy for two reasons. One, it was closer to her than Los Angeles and second, he was getting a good offer from a reputed company. Even if it was weekends they could meet and possibly once they could drive, it would be easier.

So by the New Year the newly married couple was in USA, the land of dreams for the young generation.

And, unknown to them at that moment, a new story was about to begin…

******

Chapter 11
Laxmi

Life was fast and challenging to both. But that didn't prevent Misha getting pregnant. In fact, she was happy that her child would be provided with an American passport. Her first child was a girl. They named her Laxmi. Misha's parents had come in time for delivery and her mother stayed back for a couple of months by which time Adi's mother came to take care of the baby. For some reason, Laxmi liked Adi's mother very much and was always happy to be with her even while sleeping! For Misha it was a great relief that she could be stress free while working as the baby was well taken care of. In two years' time, both Misha and Adi moved to Boston. Misha left her company and got a new position. And soon Misha got another child. Both were very happy that they had a son.

Both learned it was difficult to manage home and office together! Misha had taken three months leave after the son was born, who was named Anand. Her mother had come for the delivery and stayed on for almost five months, by which time Adi's mother came. More than anyone else Laxmi was extremely happy and she told her grandmother she would not allow her to go back or she had to take her to India!

Unlike thousands of Indians, Aditya received his green card within two years and soon he obtained his US citizenship too. It became easier for Misha to obtain her US citizenship.

As soon as she received her US passport, she started pushing her parents to come over to the US. She managed to get admissions for her sister and brother in US Colleges.

Aditya had been doing extremely well professionally and for his age had reached a covetable position in the company hierarchy. He had come to India a few times for work and used the opportunity to visit his home. After six years when his mother was returning from US, he decided to take a couple of weeks off to accompany her and stay in the village. Laxmi insisted that she also wanted to travel with her grandmother. Misha was not very keen but Aditya made her change her mind. For Laxmi it was a tremendous change after the busy city life she had seen. The beautiful plants, rain and the tremendous love of her grandparents made a lasting impression on her mind. And though very small she saw how relaxed and a happy person her father was when he was with his parents.

"Dad, I like this place better than Boston. Can we stay here!?" Laxmi asked the day they were returning to US.

"Your mother will not like it."

"Ma has Andy (Anand)!"

"But I need you," Adi smiled and said.

"You also come here."

"Then where will we get money to have food, clothes?"

"Grandpa can give us money."

Small children had their logic. Adi smiled and said, "We will see."

Besides the grandparents, Aditya's two sisters who stayed not too far from them were very close to Laxmi. Their children were almost of the same age and little older. Both sisters had one daughter each. Laxmi's English and their Malayalam made life very interesting for everyone. Laxmi was fortunate that either her father or her mother would come home to India every year after their first trip. Misha had the strange feeling that Laxmi was getting a little too attached to Adi's family. During one of her trips, Laxmi went with her grandmother to the school where she helped the school management. After retiring from her duties, she still made it a practice to go often to the school and help teachers, students and management. Laxmi was surprised by the meagre facilities of the school but was happy as she was petted and pampered by teachers as she was the granddaughter of Mrs. Menon. Village schools have their own charm…

Life moved on…Misha was moving up. She changed a couple of companies. As she moved up, she had less and less time to spend with children. Though Adi was also in a high position, he stayed on in the same company. And he had more time with family.

One evening Adi was alone in the house. He had come a little early from work. He was sitting with a cup of coffee. When Laxmi came back from school, she was a little surprised.

"Wow! Something wrong in your office!? Or is everything OK with you!? Anyway I am so happy that I am going to have some good time with you alone, for a change. Let me run up and have a quick wash." She ran up.

Anand was at the Tennis clinic and he would be back with Misha, who after office would pick him up.

"Daddy, the other day, I overheard a conversation between two of my friends. They were commenting about a girl who is always showing off. Her father is a deputy CEO of some reputed company. And they were commenting that, you, my father, was one of the top shots in the city, younger but much higher than their friend's father. And I had much more right to show off. And here at home, Mummy acts as if she is on top of the world and you sit in one corner!!!"

"Laxmi, your mother is in a covetable position for her age. You should be proud of her."

"Daddy, this is why I admire you. I am not going to explain…You know it…But mummy expects so much from both of us children. And I am least interested in top ranks or fancy careers. I am still thinking…there are two African-American boys in our class. They are funded by some charity organization. No one goes to them apart from me and a couple of my friends. They are so poor and they keep to themselves mostly. Sometimes when we get something from cafeteria we share with them. They are actually surprised when we do this as no one shares anything with them. Fortunately they are good in their studies and so the teachers are getting along with them…

"Psychology is interesting for me. I am sure Mummy will be upset with me. She expects me to be a data analyst or something like that. Another thing in my mind is to go to India. I am debating that in my mind."

"My darling daughter, you think over everything. One should be responsible for one's decisions. I can always guide you…Now you go and do your work while I go to the gym."

At the age of 13 Laxmi made a shocking announcement one day while they were having dinner.

"Mummy, I am bored with this fast pace of life and this mechanical life. I want to go to India and take up studies there. I may lose some years. But I am gonna go for it."

"You are absolutely mad. You have a bright future here. Both of us are in a good position and can help you to do what you want to do. I don't want you to go. Adi, you please make her understand." Misha was visibly upset.

"Mummy, your happiness is not mine. For your comfort, I will try out this for six months. If I find it OK, I will continue. If not, I will come back. Please do not try to fight with me. I know what I want." She left the table.

"Adi, please talk to her and put some sense into her!"

"Misha, let us not make an issue which will make matters worse. Give her time."

"You are spoiling her." Misha also left the table. Father and son were quiet and had their dinner.

******

They landed at Mumbai airport in the morning and were waiting for the flight to Kerala. There was an announcement, "This is the last and final call for flight ES 312 to Hyderabad. Passengers are requested to board the flight immediately through gate 4." One lady was running with a girl. Adi saw them and he was not sure whether the lady was Nitya. He called out, "Nitya." She didn't turn back though the girl turned and looked. But they were in a hurry. Later in the aircraft, the daughter asked, "Mummy, why didn't you check who was calling you."

She did not reply for some time. "I didn't want to be sad." Nitya finally replied.

"So you knew who was calling. Was it my father!?"

"He sounded like that."

"That was not fair. We could have at least got his address. Now at last I know he is in India. Let me try."

She didn't say anything but her eyes were full.

******

"Daddy, did you know that lady? The girl with her looked back."

"I thought she was a girl I knew when I was in college. I am not sure."

"She looked quite cute with her tall athletic body."

"The lady or the girl!?"

"Daddy, the girl."

"Even the lady was a good sports person, if that was my friend."

******

Nearly six months passed since the incident at the airport. One day Nitya told Arathi, I want to take a trip to Kerala and visit a few places including temples.

Arathi guessed that her mother had other ideas in her mind. But she was not sure.

"When do you want to go? Will grandma be coming?"

"All of us will go. Though I do not know whether she will visit any temples. Your vacation is near. So we will plan at that time."

******

Chapter 12
Arathi and Laxmi

Being a senior officer in the AG's office, Nitya had no difficulty for accommodation. They went to Trivandrum first and Nitya went to her school and college. All her friends had left the place. She went past the engineering college.

"Your father studied in this college." The chance remark by the grandmother startled Arathi. She thought she saw her mother's eyes were full. Nitya had her dark glasses on. But a drop of tear could be seen below the dark glasses. Arathi didn't ask any question.

Next day they drove down to Kochi. In the evening, Nitya told her mother that she would go to Guruveyan temple with Arathi. She dressed up in the traditional Kerala way while Arathi wore a frock and blouse. They went to the temple. Being a rainy season and evening, there was not a big crowd. And Nitya's office in Trivandrum had informed the security about her visit and she had no difficulty. While they were waiting for the door to open, Arathi felt someone was watching her. A girl with an elderly lady was standing a few feet away. She was saying something to the lady while watching her. Arathi spoke to her mother. "I think that girl knows us. Let me go and check with her!"

"No, Arathi, I have not seen them."

Arathi just went to her and smiled.

"I felt I saw you at the Mumbai airport some time back. I am not sure."

"I am also not sure. But I thought there was another gentleman with you at that time," Arathi replied.

"This is my grandmother. My father has gone back to States."

Just at that moment the door opened and they had to move. And the security guys took them both ahead. And they could not meet again though Arathi waited outside for some time.

Nitya was a little too quiet after hearing what happened. "I think we will return to Hyderabad tomorrow. I will get the tickets changed."

"We have a few more days. Why are you in a hurry, Mummy?"

"I don't know, Arathi. But I do not feel like staying any longer."

Arathi felt it had more to do with the events in the temple and she didn't press her mother.

The next day they got the ticket changed and flew back.

Nitya's mother was also surprised.

Arathi felt her mother was a little off colour.

******

After the temple visit, Laxmi's thoughts moved in a different direction. First it was the feeling that the girl resembled a little like herself. Second was the fact that her father had tried to stop the lady who should be her mother at the airport. And then she had this feeling that her father was not that happy though he always tried to be right and friendly.

Who was this girl and why was her father interested in meeting her mother. She was almost sure that it was her mother. She felt a little sad for her father for no reason! And at that moment she took a decision. She sat down to write a mail to her father.

"I had told you I would try for six months and then decide on my future course. I have decided to continue my studies here in India. I can cope up with the studies and grandmother and grandfather are always guiding me and encouraging me and with their support, I am sure I would do very well in my studies. And I find the atmosphere far more peaceful and homely than in Boston…"

Laxmi felt happy and relaxed after she sent the mail. She knew her mother would be upset. She had copied the mail to her also.

And as expected her mother was very upset and told her not to be foolish. Father told her to wait till they meet and discuss about it. He wrote to her that they were planning to come down soon for a week.

Laxmi felt it was good that the meeting would be in India. But she sent a mail to her father asking him to do the necessary formalities so that she could stay in India. She also mentioned that she was expecting a storm!!!

******

Arathi once again decided to try her luck with Facebook. She checked Aditya Menon. This time she knew he was in USA. Once again she found quite a few Aditya Menons. But there was one with two children and had a daughter. But the photograph was a formal one and she was not sure whether he was the same person she had seen at the airport. But she found out the name of daughter was Laxmi Menon. Once again the photograph was a very old one and she could not be sure. But she felt that this could be the person she had been looking for. And another thing she felt was that if it was her father, he had not lost his feelings and regards for her mother. She did not mention any of this to her mother as she felt her mother was still in love with him.

******

It was indeed a storm. And it was sheer coincidence that both Aditya's mother and father had gone out when it happened. Misha was furious and she blamed Adi for bringing Laxmi to this godforsaken village! Laxmi tried to intervene but Misha was obstinate. She said Laxmi should leave with her the next day. Adi was quiet till that time, but when it came to this, he said it was not her decision but Laxmi's decision. On this note, the argument took an ugly turn. Misha said, "If you both don't leave tomorrow then I think I may have to rethink about her relationship."

"Amma, you are going beyond the limit. It's not such a major issue that you are talking about breaking up a family. You are taking this up as an ego problem."

"Don't advise me. I do not need your counselling or anyone's support. I am my own person. I am leaving to Kochi and I will fly out tomorrow. If you have a change of mind, you can call me."

She took her bags and walked to the car and told the driver to take her to Kochi. The driver was shocked seeing her brusque manner. All this happened in such a short time.

Aditya was calm. Laxmi sat close to him holding his hand.

"Laxmi, what do you want to do? I don't want to be the reason for you to be separated from your mother. You can fly out with her tomorrow. I will take you to Kochi."

"How about you, Daddy?"

"Probably I will have to spend some time on my own to think over quite a few things. I do not want to be hasty."

"Daddy, my decision now is never to return to States. This is what USA does to people. Here with my grandma and grandpa, I am learning the true values of life. And I don't want to lose this opportunity. And I like the atmosphere and people. We will go in the evening and meet Mummy and try to reason with her."

"I don't think it will work, my sweet daughter," replied Adi. "Anyway, we will go."

******

While they were in the car, Laxmi called her mother to find out exactly where she was staying.

"Mummy, where are you? In the airport hotel or outside?"

"So, your better sense prevailed, I am happy. Hope you have packed up all your clothes. You may not be coming back here for quite some time. I am in room no. 2 in the airport hotel."

"OK Mummy, we will speak when we meet!"

"Mummy thinks I am going back with her. She will be bitterly disappointed and upset. Wonder what is going to be the scene."

"I think it is better I stay back and you meet her. She will be able to talk to you in a more calm atmosphere," Adi told her.

"Daddy, you come up to the room a little later. I don't want her to feel that you do not want to meet her for any reason."

They reached the airport and she went up to the room. When Misha opened the door and didn't see any bag with her, her face changed. "Why did you come? I didn't need any farewell!"

"Mummy, I am no more a child. I am in high school. And I like the place and both grandma and grandpa are so caring and loving. Above all, I do not like the artificial life in the States. And another thing, Daddy likes to move over to India. So in the long run, don't you think it would be better for me to get my education here? Besides both of you studied here and managed to get good jobs in the States. So if I want, I can also get a good position when the time comes."

"Laxmi, let me make it quite clear to you. I do not intend to move to India and if Daddy wants to move then it is his decision. After that what happens I do not know. And times are changing. It is not the same when we moved to the States. You may find it a different ball game. I thought you would have better judgment than your daddy. I know he is the reason for this and probably that is the reason he didn't come with you." As she said this, there was a knock on the door and Adi entered!

"Mummy, Daddy has no part in it. In fact, he told me that he would not get involved in this and the decision was solely mine. And as I told you, I have US citizenship and any time I feel unhappy here, I can come over. So give me time."

"So when are you planning to move to India, Adi. I didn't know you have this plan. You do not discuss such a serious step with me. No wonder the daughter is like this!"

"I have not decided. My boss asked me whether I would take over as CEO of our India operations. I haven't given my decision. It is a good opening."

"If you have to move then you will have to do it alone. I don't think I will be ready to move back." Misha said.

"Anyway, we have time to think over. Let us wait. You have a safe flight back. I will be there next week. Laxmi, I will be in the restaurant down, waiting for you." Adi walked out of the room.

******

Adi returned to the States and met his boss and expressed his intention to take up the opening in India as the country head. CEO was really happy that a person who had worked in that region and knew the conditions there was taking up the position. While in Dubai, he was assigned to Mumbai quite a few times. And Adi was US staff working in India which would help him to earn quite a hefty amount and other benefits. He was happy that Laxmi could have a good break in between with him. And Adi was posted to Hyderabad which was the head office for India. Adi told Misha about the latest developments. Misha was relieved that he would still be a US employee. But she was not sure whether this assignment would be short one or long one. And Misha herself was moving up and her parents felt that Adi should look for a new opening in the US. With his experience it should not be a problem, they told Misha. Misha brought that up to Adi. "Misha, I would rather you leave the job and be with me. You have your US passport. And with my US salary it would not be any problem to have a good life. And you can yourself find a good opening sooner than later."

"I have no intention of returning to India and taking up anything there. I am pretty happy with life and my work here."

"Please think about it."

"I have nothing to think, I am a US citizen and I would be here till I die."

They didn't have any conversation that night and life was not the same after that with both being polite to each other but there was no warmth.

Adi left for India by the end of the month.

******

Arathi and Laxmi were both trying to find the connection with each other. Arathi knew that her mother was not coming out with her feelings or thoughts and she was almost sure that the person at the airport was her father. Laxmi felt that Arathi was in some way connected with her father. Both were on the social media and had been trying to connect the dots in between.

One day Arathi decided to send a friend request to Aditya Pillai who had this daughter resembling Laxmi. She didn't get a reply. Little did she know that Adi was not a great social media person and rarely opened his FB page. But Laxmi happened to see the request much later while she was with her father and both were looking for something on the FB. She didn't mention it to her father but later looked for Arathi and sent her a message. And she received a reply.

Laxmi saw the friend request when she and Adi were looking for something in the FB page of Adi. Though Adi didn't bother, Laxmi sent a friend request to Arathi just to check which girl/lady wanted to be friends with her father!

Arathi, though surprised, accepted and asked who she was as she didn't have any friend by that name!

Laxmi replied saying that she wanted to know who was Arathi who wanted to be friend with her father!

"I am searching for my father since years. The only information I have is the name Aditya Pillai and he is an engineer with an MBA. I know it is a wild goose chase. But I do not blame my father. My mother told me he had come in search of her a number of times but by sheer coincidence or bad luck, they missed each other. You may be thinking how is this possible for a husband and wife to miss each other…That can wait…my father studied in an engineering college in Trivandrum…”

“…by a curious coincidence the information matches with information I have…but before going further, let us have a little more discussion to confirm the veracity.” Laxmi wrote.

“…I do not want to create any family issues in your family. I am happy that I have a real father. It is not his fault. He tried to find my mother. But when he could not, he moved on with this life. I have no right to spoil the lives of another family. So I think we should close this matter with this. I have one last question. Did you and your father come to Mumbai a few months back?” Arathi wrote back.

“…yes, we were in Mumbai. And at the airport an incidence happened where my father thought that he recognized a lady who was rushing to catch a flight as a long lost friend from his college days…Now I am connecting the dots. Are you the same person who met me at the Guruvayur temple?!!”

“…yes. My God!”

“You are such a genuine person who is ready to sacrifice your rights for another family’s happiness. I think we should be the ones doing that. I think we should know about each other a little more before we decide on the future course of action. Don’t you agree?” Laxmi wrote.

“…now, you are being kind to me!!! Yes, let us get to know each other,” Arathi replied. For the next couple of weeks both the girls were in touch with each other and the mutual love and respect grew as days passed. Laxmi’s decision to move to India more than solidified. And she joined her grandparents in Kerala and joined the school.

******

Chapter 13
Father Daughters!

About a couple of months later, Arathi informed Laxmi she was being posted to Oman as an education consul at the Indian Consulate. And Laxmi told her that her father was in Dubai for a few months on some assignment.

On a short break from school, Laxmi joined her father in Dubai. She had not been to Dubai and she was excited to visit the place. One day after visiting a lovely beach, both father and daughter were sitting at home having time late in the evening.

"Daddy, are you happy? I feel you are putting on an act in front of all."

"Laxmi, what a question to ask after such a lovely day! What prompted you to ask such a question. Did I do something wrong or say something?"

"Exactly, for me I cannot ask for a better person than you to be my father. I have tried my best to find a fault in you. I have failed. But at the same time I have this feeling that you are not happy. You are the exact opposite of my mummy. She, her sister and brother are people who are exactly suited for the present society. And you, a complete misfit. Sometimes I wonder how you have become so successful. It gives me confidence and hope that truth and simplicity can still work. Compliment that with hard work and sincerity, that is my father. But, at times I see you sitting and staring into nothingness. Those rare moments I feel you are far away. Can I ask you a question? That day at Mumbai airport you called out for a lady. Who was she? Was she your friend? If it was, who was she? Daddy, I am born and brought up in the States. I am not that simple," she smiled.

He didn't speak for a long time. Laxmi didn't pester him nor did she speak. She sat there looking through a magazine…

"Laxmi, certain events in life cannot be explained. I am a human being and I am not perfect. So long back when I was in college I had met a girl from a very poor family but extremely brilliant. She was in school and I was in engineering college. You may call it sympathy or crush, I was attracted to that girl and our friendship got a little deep and what should not happen, happened. And I had to leave as I had completed my course and had to move to North India for my MBA. By some strange coincidence though I tried quite a few times, I could not find her. First she had moved out and later she was not in town whenever I went searching for her. So I am not sure whether the lady at the airport was the same."

"Daddy, I am so happy that you are true and frank. Now, let me tell you something! I always felt that you were trying to be right at all times especially with family. It is not from the heart. I think you are you only with me, that to 75%! And after the airport incident I started thinking that you were searching for someone. And later, circumstances or fate I happened to see the girl and her mother again. Yet another chance that we became FB friends. I am leaving tomorrow. But I want you to know that I will never feel bad if you have to leave my mother for someone whom you really love. You have given me everything and stood by me every time I was in a situation. The girl or lady I am friends with is 'Arathi'. If you come across her again, I think you should talk to her and find about her mother. I do not want to get into a conversation with her on this topic as it may hurt her because it is a very sensitive topic. Hope you are not upset with me for being frank."

"Not at all, my darling daughter. You are a little too mature for your age. But I won't deny the gist of your conversation or comments. Life is strange and it has its twists and turns. Yes, I have tried all my life to do the right things and say the right things. So if God has something else for me planned, I will wait for it. Let us leave it at that. Now let's go out and have some dinner, you have an early morning flight."

******

A few months later on another visit to Dubai, Adi was in the sports club. On the notice board was something which caught his attention.

"Dubai Tennis Tournament Final…"

Chief Guest, "Ms. Arathi Pillai, Consul Education, S.O."

He went to the office of the Club Secretary. Being a top CEO of a company which sponsored a lot of events in the club and being a longstanding member, Adi was well respected.

"Who is the Chief Guest and how come she is coming here as she is not from this country?"

"Sir, she is an excellent tennis player. Though very young we understand she is an excellent officer and a good speaker."

"Would it be possible for me to get a few minutes to meet her, when she comes?"

"Not a problem, Sir. She comes at 3:00pm for watching the finals and will be here till 6:00pm. The match starts at 3:30pm. So we will arrange before that."

"Thank you."

******

On that day, Adi had reached an hour earlier. It proved providential as Arathi reached by 2:30pm. The president of the club was yet to come. So the secretary took Adi to the chairman's room and introduced. "Madam, we would like you to meet Mr. Aditya Pillai, a very old member of our club. He was out of the country for a long time. But his US based company is a sponsor for various activities of the club."

"Mr. Aditya, Miss Arathi Pillai, a diplomat and a great tennis player. Both of you come have a chat by the time I get some coffee."

"Where are you from, Miss Menon?"

"I am from a small fishing village in Trivandrum, Kerala, and my mother's name is Nitya. Incidentally, she had a very close friend by the name Aditya!"

91

Aditya's eyes filled to the brim – he didn't speak for quite some time. "Can I meet you at the Consulate tomorrow?"

"I will fly out tonight."

"I think it would be better if you wait for me and we drive out together after the function. My flight is at 8:30 and we will sit at the airport restaurant."

"I will wait. Aditya left. Everyone was surprised that Adi left so fast. He had an urgent call and had to leave. But he would return before I leave." Arathi told the Secretary and the President.

******

Adi reached an hour before the scheduled closing of the function. Function also ended a little early. Adi told the president that he could drop Arathi to the airport as he was leaving that way. They didn't have to send a driver for that. Arathi also said she would not mind.

Adi had a yellow Corvette and he brought the car to the porch. Arathi was a little surprised as it was a coupe but she didn't show it and as the secretary opened the car, she got in. A couple of bouquets were there which Adi took and placed them in the back seat. They left.

"I am not in a hurry and this is a God-sent opportunity. Being a weekend I could even fly out tomorrow. But I may have to go to the airport to change the reservation."

"It is very simple. Just let me have the PNR number and I would do it." Adi parked the car on the side and called up his travel agent. And in a few minutes he got the ticket changed to the next day afternoon.

"Now where do you want to go? I stay in a furnished apartment. Or if you prefer I would take you to a hotel."

"Just a minute, let me call my boss the CG and inform him that I would be out till tomorrow." Arathi called up and informed that she was staying back to spend some time with a relative of her.

"Let us go to a quiet place and talk and then decide for the rest of the day, "Arathi suggested.

Adi drove to a top of the line hotel and they chose a very cozy corner in the coffee shop.

"Where is your mother and what is your father doing?"

"My mother is a *single mother*. And if i trust my mother, you are my father. I do not blame you in any way. Because the cruel and bitter game is the result of bad timing and fate. My mother knew you tried to contact her a number of times but the timing was completely against her. And then her situation was not that luxurious that she could fly or travel in search of you. And I was brought up by the heroic mother of mine. But being very smart she obtained a birth certificate for me, where she recorded 'Aditya Pillai' as my father.

"And she was very studious and smart to get through her IAS exam. And today she is a very senior officer in the AG's office at Amravati near Hyderabad. That in a nut shell is our story.

"I will add a couple more paragraphs to my story. It seems to me fate is trying to make up for the cruel things it did. I would not be sitting here and talking to you today but for your daughter or rather my stepsister Laxmi. She is such a sweet, sensible girl. From the long chats we had over the last few months, I have a feeling that somewhere down in your heart, you still love my mother. Despite all the success in your career and with all the money you made and are making, you seem to be a lonely person. This is what I understood from Laxmi.

"It was overwhelming and highly stressful moment for a girl to meet a person whom she thinks is her father but with no proof other than the circumstantial coincidences. I know in this modern era possibly a DNA test may or may not prove. But it is the emotional connect which is more crucial. I have been talking and you have not touched your coffee yet."

Adi sipped his coffee and was silent for some time. "Arathi, you speak about your state of mind now, do you know what is going through my mind. I am numb. After nearly 25 years I am reconnected with my past. And I do not even know whether I will be rejected or accepted. But I will tell you this; I do not care for any position or wealth if I am able to be with your mother. I will take my chance and accept whatever the fate has decided for me…

"Now can I ask you this, would you like to spend the night in my apartment?"

"I think it may be better than a hotel room alone, "Arathi replied.

"There is a shop in the apartment complex selling clothes and other essentials. I know you didn't plan to spend a night here. So if you do not mind, I want you to get a few clothes and other things for the night and let me as a father pay for it."

They were in the car. "You are very thoughtful," replied Arathi. Arathi didn't expect to see a 7 star complex when Adi mentioned that he was staying in an apartment complex. It was a very luxurious complex with a hotel, office block and apartment complex. It had quite a few high-end shopping outlets and beauty salons, etc. Arathi got whatever she needed for the night and as insisted by her father got another dress for the next day. The apartment facing the sea was on the 30th floor and there was a large balcony with a swing and quite a few seats. As he opened the door, there was a strong breeze. Adi showed Arathi the guest room and told her to freshen up while he changed.

Adi got a glass of water and an orange juice for Arathi and he got himself a glass of sparkling water. They both sat down in the balcony.

"It's such an amazing site from this height," Arathi said.

"I use this apartment mainly for sleeping in the night. My office is in the office complex. So most of the time I spend there," Adi told her.

"Arathi, life is a most unpredictable phenomenon. No astrologer in the world can predict what is in store for you. As the saying goes, man proposes God disposes. We plan, think and decide in our minds that these are the things we would do, but more often than not, things go awry and we land up somewhere where we never thought would find ourselves. I have tried all my life to be true to myself and do and say whatever is right. I have been misunderstood, yelled at, ostracized but I have maintained my stand. Probably I am successful in my career because my employees trust me and have faith in me. Laxmi being your friend would have told you about my life. She is more than a daughter to me. She is different and sometimes I feel she has more or less the same principles as mine.

"I can't tell you how happy I feel today sitting with you. Your mother is one of a kind. I admired her from the day I met. To achieve what she has is no ordinary feat. That I couldn't be part of her story is a quirk of fate.

"Looking at you, I remember her basketball days! Being my daughter, not able to hug you, makes me even sadder."

Arathi, who was sitting silently and looking, suddenly got up and walked up to Adi. She sat on his lap, hugged him and started crying.

Adi's eyes were full to the brim but he controlled and just held her tightly. She was still crying…

******

It was quite late when they went down to the hotel coffee shop and ordered sandwiches and juice. And it was midnight when they returned and Adi led her to the guest room and sat on the sofa.

"Arathi, please tell me how to reach your mother? Please do not call her and tell her about our meeting till I meet her. I want her reaction first hand! And I will call you and tell you what happened. If God is kind to me, my Nitya will accept me."

"I have no doubts in my mind. And I will be taking leave and would be there the day after."

"OK, my sweet daughter. Now you rest. Good night."

Adi closed the door and moved to his bedroom.

Arathi didn't sleep. She got on to her mobile phone and checked for Laxmi in the FB. She had mentioned to her that she was meeting her father that evening. And Laxmi was online! They chatted for quite some time and Arathi told her she would be flying down to Cochin and she wanted Laxmi to meet her and accompany her. Laxmi had to convince her grandparents that she needed to go to Hyderabad.

******

Chapter 14
Homecoming

Adi and Arathi both were up early. They went down for breakfast and decided to go to the airport and check whether Adi could catch a flight to India. Arathi said she would spend her time in the airport if Adi's flight was early. They reached the airport by 10 and Adi could catch a flight to Mumbai at 11:30. He could probably reach Hyderabad by 7 and Amaravati by 8 if all went well. And Adi having no luggage other than a handbag could manage the connection at Mumbai and reached Amaravati by 8:30. As he had the address he went straight to the bungalow. It was not easy at that time to convince the security that he was a family friend. Security called the house and said there was a gentleman who said he was a friend of Arathi and was coming from the Middle East. Nitya told the security to let him in. He reached the home and the door was opened by a maid and told him that the lady of the house will come in a few minutes. Adi walked to a cabinet on the side which had quite a few photographs.

"Yes, what can I do for you?"

Adi turned around.

It was a moment of silence!

There was no conversation!

She was standing only a few feet away!

Adi extended his hand, "You can refuse my hand, Nitya, I will never blame you. But you can accept my hand and I will NEVER leave you till my death."

Her eyes were full as she moved closer. The embrace was a very long one. They didn't speak. She held him and walked him to the guest room and closed the door. It was as if she was the school girl and had never left him. It was pain and pleasure!

There was a soft knock on the door, "Nitya, Nitya…"

Nitya got up, she walked up to the door and said, "Mummy, you have your dinner and go to sleep. I will speak to you in the morning. Don't ask me anything now," she spoke very softly.

She went back to the bed. Slowly she started wearing her jeans and t-shirt. The night lamp was casting a shadow. She looked at Adi. He was sound asleep. She covered him very softly with the sheet. She thought, if he is to sleep so deeply, he must be feeling very safe and calm. And to feel that way he should be happy. And how did he find this house? His shirt and pants were on the floor. She picked them up and was about to hang them when a few papers and cards fell off from the shirt's pocket. And one card had the government of India emblem. She read, "Arathi Pillai, Consul…"

Her face lit up with a smile and she moved onto the bed and got under the sheet.

******

Adi was tired with the long travel and also with the tension and apprehension in mind. And when both of them fell into each other's arms, time stopped. And the release of tension and the happiness of the union were enough for him to sleep like a baby. And when slowly he opened his eyes, Nitya was also sleeping with her arms and legs on him. He didn't move nor wake her up. He just went on looking at her face which was exactly the same as long back. She hadn't changed. *She must have been keeping herself healthy by workouts or sports*, he thought.

She just moved. "My sweet girl, will you take me back?" He pulled her close.

"You must have heard the whole story from Arathi. But I don't know where you are and what situation you are in. How can I answer that question."

"My question is simple. Will you take me back?"

"If my daughter has given you the address to find me that means she has accepted you. So the answer is quite easy. If you need me, I am yours."

Their locked lips didn't allow further conversation.

It was quite some time before there was any conversation. In fact, Nitya started crying. In between a few words would come out. "You don't know how difficult it is for a single mother to survive…let alone, dealing with society."

Adi didn't speak; he just hugged her close to him and wiped her tears with his lips often. It was almost an hour before she became calm.

"My sweet darling, I am famished. I had a sandwich in the morning! Can you give me some water first!?" Adi murmured in her ears.

"Oh! Sorry! Your bag is in the drawing room. You wash your face and freshen up while I get your bag." She moved out while Adi went inside the bathroom. Adi changed into his night dress and came out. Nitya went inside the kitchen, got a glass of water and got two plates with some rotis and curry. Both of them sat down on the dining table and had dinner.

"Adi, I have been talking all this time. And you have met Arathi and she must have given you our life story. Now you tell me where I stand in your life!"

Adi told Nitya about his search for her and his life and career and about his children. He also told about the connection between Laxmi and Arathi.

"Nitya, it might take a while. But from this moment you are my responsibility and thanks to God I am based in Hyderabad. I travel to Dubai, Singapore and Middle East regularly. Let us discuss about it in the coming days."

Both of them got up and washed up and sat for a few minutes. "You have a choice. Either you can sleep in the guest room or you can come up with me," she spoke with a smile.

"I don't think I would want to waste even a minute. It has been quite long since the college." They walked up the stairs.

"Since I am not married, I have no ethical problem. But your case is different," Nitya said while climbing up the steps.

"For the society, I am married to Misha. But in my heart there is only one person and finally I have reached her. Let us leave it at that for the time. I wonder what your mother is going to feel and react."

"You leave that to me." They entered the bedroom.

******

Being one of the few IB schools in the state, admission was difficult due to the high quality standards and high strength of students. Even then Laxmi, granddaughter of Mrs. Pillai, managed to find a seat for herself. She took French for her language class and at home Mrs. Pillai arranged a Malayalam teacher. She was an intelligent and hard working girl and with her US based training she managed to get through the initial phase of adjustment without much difficulty. And as the time progressed she proved to be a brilliant student academically. Besides academics she excelled in Ballet dancing which the dance teacher made use of by getting her to train other students. Within a short time, she became a very popular student in the school.

One day, Misha and her father had come to the school unannounced. They went to the Principal's office. Being very fashionably dressed and speaking with an accent, the Principal was a little apprehensive when they walked in.

"I am Laxmi's mother and this is her grandfather. We came this morning from Boston. Wanted to meet her. How is she?"

"She is one of the top students in the class. Also an all-round student. I will call her. You can wait in the waiting room."

Laxmi was in her uniform and was shocked to see them both in the school. "You could have called me up or sent a message. I would have come to meet you and pick you up from airport. Really surprised. How are you, Mummy?"

"How are you? You seem to be enjoying your school."

"Mummy, you should be happy that I am one of the top in a short time and also representing the school for dance, debates etc. Really, I am enjoying the school. How is my brother and his tennis?"

"Laxmi, can you take permission to come with us. We can go over to the hotel, have lunch and catch up."

"Mummy, you tell me where you stay. I will finish my classes by 3 and will meet you by 4. I will go home, wash and change. I do not like to come in the school uniform. Besides Grandpa and Grandma will be happy to meet you both. It has been quite some time since you came this side."

"Laxmi, we just dropped in for a day to meet you. We are taking the evening flight to Bangalore. Thought you would like to spend some time with us." Her voice was a little rough.

"OK Mummy, I will meet the Principal and would meet you in a few minutes!"

They spent the next few hours at the hotel. Conversation was more formal than homely. Misha had brought some classy dresses and jeans which Laxmi thought in her mind as very jazzy for the village!

Grandfather asked her, "Does your father come or is he still busy travelling around the world? Why do you have to stay like this in this atmosphere when you have such top of the line facilities with your mother and brother. The whole family is there and here you are alone. Anyway, soon you will have to make a choice."

"I am very happy here and US does not appeal to me at all." There was hardly any conversation after that. Laxmi left after hugging her mother and grandfather. "You don't have to come down. I know the car."

As she came down the lift and was passing through the reception desk, she saw a person and recognized him as the famous lawyer who had come to the school for a function. She had done the introduction speech on that day. She went up to him and wished.

"What a coincidence. I came to meet your mother for some signature. How are you?"

"Fine, thank you." And she left thinking about the signature and grandfather's comment on the choice she would have to make!!!

Laxmi couldn't convince her grandparents, especially grandmother. They said they would meet her at the airport and if everything was OK, they would buy the ticket and allow her to go. She was carrying only her overnight bag; Arathi's flight came in a little early around 8 in the morning. She came out and had no difficulty in finding Laxmi.

"These are my grandparents. I told them you were my idol and also a diplomat. But they wanted to meet you before allowing me to travel with you," Laxmi said.

"They are cent percent right. These days it is very difficult to recognize who is genuine and who is not. By the way, I have met your grandmother at the temple quite some time back. I hope she remembers, "Arathi replied.

"Yes, I do. You are too young to be diplomat. Really it's an achievement for a girl."

Arathi took her visiting card and handed it over to both of them.

"Please make sure she returns tomorrow. I will go get the tickets. Which flight are you taking, Miss Arathi?"

"Call me Arathi. Consider me just as Laxmi. I am taking the 10:30 I.A. flight."

He went and returned a few minutes later with a return ticket. "I have kept the return open." Tell me when you leave from Hyderabad. But make sure it's tomorrow.

Both Arathi and Laxmi went inside the terminal. There was more than an hour so they went to the restaurant.

"Tell me all the news with no full stop or gaps." Laxmi was eager to know.

"Life or fate, I wonder which one brought us two together. And I hope we will be together. Yesterday night your father or our father was with my mother. I do not know what has happened. We will come to know only when we reach there. But Laxmi, he is still in love with my mother, I realized."

"Arathi I told you he was doing everything right but his heart was somewhere. And I have some news which I will share with both of you when we meet. I do not know what the future is. I pray to God that you will never be separated from me."

"Laxmi you are my sister and rest assured I would do whatever is required to keep you with me. I need the help of only the all-powerful heavenly father as they say in the church!"

The flight was announced at that moment.

******

"Is there a temple nearby?" Adi asked as soon as he woke up. Nitya had already woken up and had gone down to speak to her mother. She had come up with a glass of water.

"I can drive you there as it is a little far. You finish your bath here and I will get ready by that time."

She bent and kissed him and left.

"Mummy, don't ask me any question. I have no answer. At this moment I am not thinking. I am just allowing my instincts or feelings in my heart to guide me. Arathi has met him, stayed in his home and gave him the address. If she is able to accept him as her father, then I think I should give him a chance. And finally I have no one else other than you. If one day you are not there, I don't want to be left alone as Arathi will have her life. Now let me get ready. Adi wants to go to a temple." Nitya was talking to her mother as she applied oil on her hair.

"It's your life. You do what you feel right," Mother replied.

They went to the temple and inside Adi took out a ring from his hand and put it on her finger.

"In front of my favourite Lord Krishna, I have taken you as mine!"

Nitya's eyes were full. Both prayed for some time and they left. The ring was loose on the ring finger and she changed it to another finger.

They got into the car and the phone rang.

"Ma, I have just reached India. I will reach Hyderabad before noon. I have a friend with me. Will see you for lunch."

"That was Arathi. She didn't say where she was. She will be here for lunch. Probably she wants to know what happened between us," Nitya said. "She also said she has a friend with her!"

"We can go out later and I can change the ring for you."

"No need. You were wearing it before you gave me and I want it. I will keep it. Do you want to go home or want to go for a drive around the city? It's too early for breakfast but easy for a drive around with no traffic."

"OK, at your command," Adi smiled. "But I am not dressed for getting down anywhere."

For nearly an hour she drove to different landmarks and finally returned home for a good Malayali traditional breakfast.

"Good morning, Aunty. You look almost the same with a little grey hair. I don't know what to say other than that I am there for both of you and Arathi from now on. That is my word."

"I will pray for that," replied Nitya's mother.

After the breakfast, Adi told Nitya that he would attend to some urgent office work. It would take only less than an hour. And then they could catch up on all the lost times!

She took him to the guest room where she had her office table set up.

******

He finished the work and was getting up when Nitya walked in. Both of them sat on the bed. Adi got her head on his lap and softly kissed on her lips.

"I am thinking of Arathi. And why would she bring a friend when she knows you are here. I am a little anxious or rather tensed." She got up from the bed and sat on the sofa opposite the bed. "Tell me, Adi, how is it possible for you to leave your wife and your work in US. You should know that I have lived my life alone for such a long time and now I have Arathi for support. I don't want you in any kind of problem.

Now I know you are there and I could call you any time I need…" Adi got up and put his hand on her mouth.

"You don't have to make me feel more depressed. Finally I have made it to you and I have no intention of losing my precious gem. What I am planning to do is to go to my office to get everything organized and by next weekend come and take you to my home in Kerala and introduce you to my parents and especially to Laxmi. Laxmi played a major part to bring us together. She need not have contacted Arathi or told me about her. I am sure you would like her. Why are you again crying? I am here and you should be smiling," Adi pulled her up and hugged her.

"It is the happiness of finding you after so many years." The phone rang. Nitya moved to pick it up.

"Mummy, we are in Hyderabad. Will see you soon." It was Arathi on the phone.

******

All three of them were standing on the terrace when the car horn sounded. The gate keeper opened the gate. Arathi was paying off the taxi.

"Oh! My God, it is Laxmi," Adi just ran off.

"What a contrast, one fair American girl and the other a dark Indian one. I wonder," Nitya's mother commented.

"My good mother, she is an Indian girl with a fair complexion. And if you really look at them, they have some resemblance somewhere. And mind you those two girls are the reason why I am smiling today. Let us go down." Nitya told her mother.

Adi hugged Laxmi and then Arathi. He held Laxmi's hand. "Wow! I am overwhelmed with shocks and surprises since last two days. How did you both manage to come together?"

"Modern day communication and travel make everything possible. I was in Kochi this morning to pick my sweet sister," Arathi told him.

Nitya and her mother had come down. Laxmi bent and touched both their feet. "Amma, that's your American girl," Nitya had a smile on her face.

She hugged her and then Arathi.

"My mother was saying this fair girl looked very American." Nitya said.

"Grandma, Laxmi is American may be by complexion and her English but at heart a true Malayali more than an Indian. Such a sweet heart she has," Arathi told her grandma.

"You must be completely tired. Go and wash your face and have something to pep you up."

"I don't know what to call you, for the time being let me call you aunty. Arathi is more than a sister to me. She is kind of an idol for me. What a great person she is at this young age. So proud of her. I told her I am going to call her chechi, now that I know she is really a sister of mine." Laxmi's pronunciation was typically American though she was trying her best to sound like everyone else.

Both Arathi and Laxmi went in to freshen themselves while Nitya and her mother moved into the kitchen.

"She seems like a good girl."

"Amma, it is not 'seems like', she is a good girl. I am really surprised," Nitya replied.

They all sat down on the dining table.

Adi was between both the girls.

"You have a lovely bungalow aunty and what a garden," Laxmi said.

"Nitya is a senior government servant with security, etc. Every rich guy in town is scared of her. Because she has all the information," Adi told Laxmi.

"Mother and daughter both seem to be two people to be admired," Laxmi commented.

"I haven't seen my father so happy since a very long time. Feel so exhilarated that I could finally trace you, Aunty. But if not for Arathi, nothing would have been possible. I am also so happy for my father. Anyway, Daddy, I have some news for you. Some may call it bad but I think for you it should be good. After lunch we will discuss. First I want only Daddy and Arathi. After that it is for them to decide how and what to say." There was an atmosphere of suspense!

******

"Daddy, yesterday I received a call from my grandpa in New York. He asked me to pack up and return to Boston as Mummy was thinking of a separation. Because all of them feel that you would like to stay in India. And Grandpa, Grandma and my brother, sister besides Mummy, all are happy to be in States. And with your work being in India and the Middle East, it is going to be long gaps. So they all feel that a separation may be better. I told him that I did not want to discontinue my studies right at this moment and will discuss my views when I go there for summer vacation. I don't think he liked it but he didn't say anything. I think it kind of will release some tension from your mind. Sometimes, time and fate play the game."

Both Arathi and Adi didn't speak for some time.

"As the politician says, no comments," were the only words from Adi.

Arathi was thoughtful.

"Daddy, I have to catch the last flight back to Kochi. Only on that condition I could come here. Arathi didn't tell them that I would be meeting you or you are here. So after some time you leave me to the airport," Laxmi told her father.

They went round the house and chatted for quite some time.

While Arathi had a quick nap, both Laxmi and Adi sat with Nitya watching old albums. Laxmi was really impressed with the achievements of Arathi in both sports and academics. She was so thrilled to find that Arathi was a whiz kid!

Later they had a cup of tea and coffee.

Nitya went up with Laxmi so she could dress up.

Around 5 in the evening, Adi and Laxmi were ready to leave. Nitya and Arathi accompanied them to the airport. Aditya decided to accompany Laxmi as he didn't want her to travel alone. He went and got a ticket.

They went inside and Laxmi held Nitya's hand, "I love you, Aunty."

Nitya gave her a bear hug. "Love you too, my sweet heart." Arathi and Laxmi moved a little away and spoke something and they hugged.

Adi was holding Nitya's hand and hugged her.

Both Adi and Laxmi moved away.

Nitya and Arathi were watching both father and daughter walking away.

Watching them, both with their own thoughts!

Arathi turned to say something to her mother. She had tears running down her cheeks!

"Mummy, you should be happy. Why are you crying?"

Nitya didn't say anything for a few minutes. "Watching them, I was remembering Salman Khan walking away with that song…*Tadaptadapke is dil se aah nikaltirahi…*"

Arathi's eyes also started watering.

******

108